"We're onto him

"There's just one pro...

"What? That we probably haven't found everything?" There was one time gap big enough that they'd agreed there was probably at least one more connected crime. "I'm sure another one will surface eventually."

"Not that," Keara said. "Every single one of these cases is in a different jurisdiction. Hell, every case is in a different state."

"Okay, but   "

"Jax, he set off this bomb in Luna, left behind this symbol. This pattern suggests he commits one crime and then leaves. He's probably already gone."

He stared back at her, his grin slowly fading.

Beside her, Patches whined and nudged her leg.

They'd found the criminal's trail, but had it already gone cold here?

Boom!

A sound like thunder directly overhead exploded. Then the silence following the loud noise was replaced by screaming.

A special thanks to everyone at Harlequin for helping me bring my K-9 Alaska series to life, especially my editor, Denise Zaza, assistant editor Connolly Bottum for managing all the details and publicist Lisa Wray for sharing the stories with bloggers and reviewers. My sister, Caroline Heiter, brought her beta reading magic to this book, and my husband, Andrew Gulli, kept me fed and working! A special shout-out to my #BatSignal writer pals, especially Tyler Anne Snell, Nichole Severn, Regan Black, Louise Dawn and Janie Crouch, who brought motivation and inspiration during virtual writing sessions.

K-9 COLD CASE

ELIZABETH HEITER

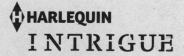

HARLEQUIN
INTRIGUE

This book is for my husband, Andrew, who gives me my own HEA every single day.

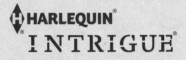

Recycling programs for this product may not exist in your area.

ISBN-13: 978-1-335-28461-7

K-9 Cold Case

Copyright © 2021 by Elizabeth Heiter

This edition published by arrangement with Harlequin Books S.A.

For questions and comments about the quality of this book, please contact us at CustomerService@Harlequin.com.

Harlequin Enterprises ULC
22 Adelaide St. West, 40th Floor
Toronto, Ontario M5H 4E3, Canada
www.Harlequin.com

Printed in U.S.A.

Elizabeth Heiter likes her suspense to feature strong heroines, chilling villains, psychological twists and a little romance. Her research has taken her into the minds of serial killers, through murder investigations and onto the FBI Academy's shooting range. Elizabeth graduated from the University of Michigan with a degree in English literature. She's a member of International Thriller Writers and Romance Writers of America. Visit Elizabeth at www.elizabethheiter.com.

Books by Elizabeth Heiter

Harlequin Intrigue

A K-9 Alaska Novel

K-9 Defense
Alaska Mountain Rescue
K-9 Cold Case

The Lawmen: Bullets and Brawn

Bodyguard with a Badge
Police Protector
Secret Agent Surrender

The Lawmen

Disarming Detective
Seduced by the Sniper
SWAT Secret Admirer

Visit the Author Profile page at Harlequin.com.

CAST OF CHARACTERS

Keara Hernandez—When a bomb goes off near Desparre, the police chief discovers a possible connection to her husband's unsolved murder. Investigating this case could bring her the closure she's wanted for seven years—or it could destroy her future happiness.

Jax Diallo—The victim specialist comes to Desparre to help the bombing victims, but he quickly becomes embedded in a side investigation with Keara. Falling for the intriguing police chief wasn't part of his plan, but he thinks solving the case could help her move on—until the bomber fixates on Keara.

Patches—The FBI therapy dog's job is to help the bombing victims, but she's just as effective with the FBI and police investigators.

Ben Nez—The FBI agent wants Jax to stick to his role—and out of the way of investigators.

Juan Hernandez—Keara's husband was killed seven years ago and when his case went cold, Keara fled to Alaska.

Rodney Brown—He might have been a witness—or even a suspect—in one of Juan's last cases, but he disappeared shortly after Juan was killed. Could that murder have been just the beginning?

Chapter One

You have to be the calm in their chaos.

Jax Diallo repeated the mantra in his head, the words he always reminded himself of when he was sent to the scene of a tragedy. Being an FBI Victim Specialist wasn't for the faint of heart.

As the FBI vehicle he was riding in slammed to a stop, Jax closed his eyes for a few seconds, tried to center himself. Tried to prepare to walk into the aftermath of a bomb.

"Let's go!" one of the Special Agents said, hopping out of the vehicle with his partner, two Evidence Response Technicians on their heels.

With the doors open, the bitter Alaskan wind penetrated the vehicle. So did the unnatural quiet of nature, as if all the animals had taken off. The silence was punctuated by staccato bursts of sobbing, from victims or family members still on the scene. Or maybe a first responder or law-enforcement officer who'd never seen anything like this.

In the distance a phone rang and rang, before going silent and then starting up again. A friend or family member searching for a loved one, desperately hoping for an answer to a call that would never be picked up.

"You ready, Patches?" Jax asked quietly.

His Labrador retriever stared up at him

steadily, the soft brown eyes that always reassured victims also working their magic on Jax. She'd transitioned fast from a scared, abandoned puppy into one of the FBI's best therapy dogs. Right now she could read his mood as well as any victim's she'd been sent to help.

He gave her a reassuring pet, then climbed out of the SUV. Twenty feet ahead the beautiful greenery of a park was littered with the twisted metal skeleton of what had probably once been a park bench. Pieces of metal had blown into the street, and were still smoldering. Directly beside the park, a small freestanding building—maybe a bathroom—had collapsed, the front wall gaping open. Crumbled concrete, support beams and insulation spilled out of it. Around the edges of the park, one tree was pierced with a metal fragment, like a spear. Others were singed black and missing huge limbs.

As Jax got closer, he saw the detritus from first responders: abandoned needle covers, wrappers and blood-soaked gauze. The concrete walkway was stained a deep red.

The scent still lingered, too, burned metal and charred trees, and something worse underneath. A scent Jax recognized from too many other crime scenes.

The bomb had gone off just over an hour ago in the sleepy town of Luna, Alaska, on an otherwise peaceful Saturday morning. When it happened, Jax had been four hundred miles away, sipping his morning coffee on his back deck, with Patches asleep at his feet. Then his FBI phone had gone off and he'd grabbed his go bag and raced to the tiny nearby airfield, where a jumper plane was waiting.

The briefing on the plane had been short and information-light. A single bomb had detonated. At least six were dead and thirteen more injured. Right now the tiny Luna Police Department had no suspects, no obvious motive and no idea whether to expect more bombs.

Jax looked around the small park, with butterfly-shaped benches around the edges and a couple of trails leading into the woods. It wasn't an obvious spot to set off a bomb. There'd been no events here, except for an impromptu soccer game. All locals, no news coverage. If the bomber had a specific target, the park seemed like an odd place to go after them, because a bomb here was too likely to miss that person and take out others. If he hadn't been targeting a specific person, it still seemed like a strange choice, without the volume of spectators that mission-oriented bombers favored.

Not your job, Jax reminded himself. The agents would search for the perpetrator. He needed to help the victims and their families.

Kneeling down, he slipped special shoes onto Patches's feet that would protect her from bomb fragments and other sharp items in the rubble. Ideally, they'd stay out of the blast zone entirely, but that wasn't always possible. Then he stood, holding his arm out straight, directing her toward the park. "Come on, Patches."

She followed his direction, walking past the gawkers on the outskirts of the scene. She headed straight toward the woman sitting alone on one of the intact benches, with a vacant gaze and blood smearing her sweatshirt. When Patches reached the woman, she sat next to her, and the woman—girl, really, Jax decided as he reached her—seemed to refocus. She reached out a shaky hand to pet Patches, who scooted closer.

Ignoring the chaos behind him as the FBI agents and evidence specialists coordinated with Luna police, Jax knelt in front of the girl. He pegged her at nineteen. The shock in her eyes suggested she still hadn't processed what had happened. The grass stains on the knees of her pants suggested she might have been part of the soccer game. Or maybe she'd skidded to the ground from the force of the blast or in desperation to help someone she loved. There were a couple of bandages visible on her arms where she'd rolled up her sleeves, but nothing that would have caused the amount of blood on her shirt.

"I'm Jax Diallo," he said softly, not wanting to startle her. "I'm a Victim Specialist with the FBI."

Her gaze skipped to his, then back to Patches.

She pet his dog faster, and Patches moved even closer, putting her head on the arm of the bench and making the girl smile.

"What can I do for you?" Jax asked. "Is there someone I can call? Do you need to get to the hospital to see someone?" He hoped the person whose blood coated her shirt wasn't in the morgue.

She glanced at him again, surprise and wariness in her eyes. "You're not going to ask me about what happened?"

"We can talk about that, too, if you want. I'm here for you. So is Patches."

Her gaze darted to his dog, at the mix of brown and black that had earned her the name, and smiled briefly.

"What's your name?"

"Akna." Her voice was croaky, quiet enough that he had to lean forward to make it out.

She'd inhaled smoke when the bomb went off. Or the blast was still impeding her ability to tell how loud she was speaking, even an hour later. Probably both.

"Akna, I'm a Victim Specialist. It's my job to help you and anyone else who needs me today or in the future. Right now that means getting you any resources you might want, or helping you contact someone."

She stared back at him, her gaze still slightly

unfocused. But as she pet Patches, the fear and confusion on her face slowly started to fade.

Most people had no idea his job existed. But he was the lifeline between victims and their families and the Special Agents, who often didn't have the time or know-how to manage victims' many needs. Part of his role was to help victims navigate the criminal justice process, making it more likely they'd find the perpetrator and put that person behind bars. But the other part was simply helping victims get the resources they needed to move on with their lives.

"Akna, were you here alone?"

"Yeah." She shook her head. "No. Sort of."

"You were here for the soccer game?" he guessed.

"Yeah. We've got an online community board. Someone wanted to play." She shrugged, a fast jerk of her shoulders. "It was a nice day. I wanted some exercise." A strangled sob broke free. "How could this happen?"

"Is there someone you want me to call? To let them know you're okay? Or to pick you up?"

"I helped carry her over there," Akna said, gesturing vaguely toward the edge of the park. "I saw a couple of the players trying to lift her, carry her away from the rubble." Her voice picked up speed, picked up volume. "She was right by the building and big pieces of it fell on her. We thought it would be better. But—"

"She was a friend of yours?" Jax asked, keeping his voice calm, letting Patches do her own work as Akna continued to pet her, probably not even aware she was doing it.

Akna shook her head. "I didn't really know her. But she was on my team." Her eyes met Jax's and instantly filled with tears. "I think she was dead before we carried her over there."

"I'm sorry, Akna."

"Who would do this?"

"We don't know yet. But we're going to find out."

"We were just playing the game. I was running down the field, heading for the goal—it was supposed to be those trees." She pointed, her hand shaking uncontrollably. "No one thought to bring a net. And then…and then, there was this huge *boom*. It was so loud I could *feel* it. I don't remember falling, but then I was on the ground and people were screaming and then…" She sucked in a violent breath.

"Akna, you're okay," Jax said softly, in the same even tone he'd used with hundreds of victims. "You're okay. It's over."

"Akna!"

Akna leaped to her feet, making Patches stand, too. The tears she'd been persistently blinking back suddenly spilled over as she whispered, "Mom."

Then a woman with the same dark hair, the

same deep-set eyes, rushed over, enveloping her in a tight hug. "I heard about the bomb. And I couldn't get a hold of you. Your phone kept going straight to voice mail."

"It broke," Akna sobbed. "I fell on it and it broke. And then I was trying to help Jenny and—"

"It's okay, it's okay," her mom soothed, smoothing back her daughter's hair. "I'll take you home."

"Akna," Jax said, holding out his card. "You call me if I can help you, okay? Anything at all. Anytime."

She took the card with a shaky hand, nodded.

Akna's mom looked at him questioningly, even as her gaze skimmed over his coat, emblazoned with *FBI*. "You're investigating the bombing?"

"I'm a Victim Specialist, not an investigator. I'm here for your daughter. If she saw anything that could help the investigation, she can talk to me. Or if she wants information about the status of the case. Or if she wants help finding someone to talk to about what happened today. The same goes for you, ma'am."

Surprise registered on the woman's face as she glanced at the card in Akna's hand, then back at him.

Akna swiped the tears off her face with the sleeve of her bloody sweatshirt, then whispered, "Thanks, Jax." Then she gave his dog a shaky smile. "Bye, Patches."

Woof!

Her happy bark made a handful of Luna police officers glance their way.

Akna let out a surprised laugh, then she left, her arm looped around her mom's waist.

Jax pulled out a notebook and jotted down the details Akna had mentioned, before tucking it back into his FBI jacket. Then he raised his arm to gesture toward the other group of civilians gathered at the edge of the park. "Let's go, Patches."

She headed toward them without pause, used to her role of calming people.

As he followed, snippets of their conversation drifted toward him.

"Why would anyone set off a bomb here?"

"…nothing here, man!"

Right now Jax needed to focus on the victims' immediate needs, on information he could gather to help them later and on the details that might matter in the investigation. But he had a background in psychology and he'd never quite been able to turn off the analytical side of his brain that sorted through why a person did the things they did. It had helped him back in his therapist days. As an FBI employee, it sometimes made him clash with the investigating agents.

But right now he couldn't stop wondering: What had a bomber been doing in this small park?

Jax had been to the sites of several bombs since

he'd joined the FBI. Usually, they fell into two categories: big spectacles meant to cause widespread panic, or small explosives meant to kill a certain person. This didn't seem like either one.

This crime scene was different from anything he'd experienced. Even though knowing the motivation behind a crime didn't necessarily make it less scary, for Jax, it made it easier to comprehend. And usually, easier to comprehend meant a starting place for him, for the victims, even for the Special Agents in their investigation.

He squinted at the destruction in this once-beautiful place and dread settled in his gut. Was the bomber finished or was he just getting started?

BEING POLICE CHIEF in a remote Alaskan town was supposed to be quiet. It was supposed to be simple.

Today Keara Hernandez had spent the day reassuring scared citizens that they were safe in Desparre, that the explosion in the town next to them was under investigation. That she'd have more information over the next few days, that it would be solved soon. She hoped her reassurances were true. But she'd been unable to get through to her colleagues in the Luna PD all day.

So now, instead of going home to rest, she was on her way down the mountain that separated Desparre from Luna. Getting to Luna was a two-hour venture if you went around the base of the mountain. Trekking up and then down the mountain again took half the time. In winter that trip could be dangerous. Right now, with May a few days away and the snow melted except in the highest parts of the mountain, it was much easier. But Keara felt every minute of the drive.

Her throat was sore after talking to more citizens in a day than she usually did in a week in her town full of recluses. Her shoulder ached from one of her regular calls, close to her own house. A belligerent drunk who liked to scream at his wife. At least once a week Keara was out there, talking him down and occasionally tossing him in a cell. Today he'd taken a run at her and she'd had to cuff him, bring him in the hard way.

She wanted to soak it off in a tub, relax in her quiet house, set apart from her neighbors by a few miles. She wanted to continue to live in the fantasy that a small town like Desparre would never face the same types of threats a big city like Houston saw.

The thought of her hometown made her chest tighten and Keara pushed it out of her mind, punched down on the gas. This was a fluke. She'd lived in Desparre for six years and although bar fights and domestic violence weren't unusual, big, complex cases were few and far between. Other than the kidnapping case that had given Desparre way more attention than it had ever wanted five years ago—and a rehash six months ago when one of the kidnappers reappeared—Desparre and its neighbor Luna were places people came to stay below the radar. Not to set off bombs.

The idea made her shudder as she navigated off the mountain and toward downtown Luna, toward the quaint little park where she'd come more than once over the past six years. The first time she'd seen it, she'd thought what a fun place it would have been to take kids. Which was irrelevant for her, since that part of her life had ended before it ever got started. But right now she prayed the park hadn't been hosting one of their toddler play groups when the bomb had exploded.

The news had reported six dead and at least thirteen injured, but they hadn't offered many more details. The hospital was keeping media out and police weren't talking, other than to say they were contacting next of kin and working with the FBI to investigate. And typical of the people who chose to live in this remote Alaskan area, the residents weren't interested in their own fifteen minutes of fame.

It had been twelve hours since the bomb went off, but Keara parked down the street, not wanting to get in the way of investigators if any were still on scene. As she hurried toward the site on foot, she pulled up the collar on her lined raincoat, wishing she'd opted for something heavier. The temperatures were already dropping into the thirties, the sun casting an array of pinks and oranges across the sky as it settled behind the trees.

Her footsteps slowed as the park came into view and the sharp scent of smoke invaded her nostrils. The front of the building housing the public restrooms was blown out, a metal bench shredded to pieces, the once-green field charred black in places. But it was the bloodstain splotches on the ground, on the benches, even on the side of the building, that made her stomach flip-flop. Made memories rush forward that she ruthlessly pushed down.

The area was cordoned off, but she didn't see any evidence markers, suggesting all the obvious evidence had already been bagged up and taken to the lab. There was likely more searching to do. Bomb fragments could fly a long distance, into the woods behind the park or buried under the rubble of the building.

Keara scanned the park, her gaze moving quickly over the civilians on the outskirts of the scene. She was looking for an officer who would give her straight information about the status of the case. All she saw was one Luna officer she didn't know and another who didn't like anyone from Desparre PD after a debacle six months ago with one of her officers. She frowned, looking for friendlier faces, but she mostly saw FBI jackets, plus a handful of people covered from head to toe in white protective gear. Evidence technicians, probably more FBI. All of them flown up the four hundred plus miles from the FBI's Anchorage field office.

Movement off to her side caught her attention and then an adorable black-and-tan dog plopped down at her feet, staring up at her expectantly. Behind the dog was a man with dark curly hair, perfectly smooth light brown skin and hypnotizing dark brown eyes. He had more than half a foot on her five-foot-six-inch frame, was probably a few years older than her thirty-five years and he wore an FBI coat.

"That's Patches," he told her, in a smooth, deep voice that would have put her instantly at ease if it hadn't made awareness clench her stomach. "And I'm Jax."

He tilted his head, and she had the distinct feeling he was cataloging everything about her.

She stood a little taller, feeling self-conscious in her civilian clothes—comfortable jeans with a warm sweatshirt under her jacket, and a pair of heavy-duty boots that could kick in a door.

"Did you know one of the victims?" he asked as Patches nudged her hand with a wet nose.

Keara smiled at the dog, petting her head as she told Jax, "No. Well, I don't know. Maybe." She cleared her throat, held out her hand. "Keara Hernandez. I'm the police chief in Desparre." She gestured vaguely in the direction of the mountain. "We're Luna's neighbors."

His eyes narrowed slightly, assessing her without any of the visible surprise she was used to from Alaskans when they heard about Desparre's female police chief. Then his big hand closed around hers, warm and vaguely unsettling. "Jax Diallo. Victim Specialist for the FBI. Patches here is a therapy dog."

"Therapy?" She looked down at Patches, who stared back at her calmly. "I assumed she was a bomb-sniffing dog."

"Nope. Patches and I are here to help the victims."

"Well, maybe you can give me some details, as a professional courtesy." She showed him her badge, just in case he thought she was lying, but he barely glanced at it. "I've got to answer to my citizens tomorrow. They want to know if they're safe."

"I can't really answer that, Keara." He drew out the *e* in her name slightly, *Kee-ra*. It was almost Southern, and it made her flash back to another case, another man, another time in her life entirely.

She'd been a brand-new patrol officer, assigned to partner up with a man who would eventually become her husband. Juan had frowned at her that first day, and although he hadn't said anything, she'd seen it all over his face. He didn't like being assigned to work with a woman.

Keara glanced away from Jax, not wanting him

to see the emotions that were hard to keep off her face whenever she thought about Juan. But when she redirected her gaze to the right, all she saw was that blood.

It was a dark smear across the concrete, nothing like the thick, pooled mess that had surrounded Juan when she'd found him behind their house seven years ago. His eyes had been open, glassy, his cheek already cold to her touch.

"Keara?"

She jerked at the feel of Jax's hand on her elbow, the concerned tone of his voice. Shaking off the memory, she forced her gaze back to the Victim Specialist. "Is there someone I can talk to about the case?"

"Not right now. But I'm here if you want to talk about—"

"Sorry. I've got to go." Keara gave Patches one last pat, then spun back the way she'd come, suddenly uncaring that she'd driven all this way and hadn't gotten any answers. Because right now what she needed most was to get out of here.

Away from the bloodstains and the bomb remnants. Away from the unexpected memories.

Hopefully, the FBI would do their job fast. Hopefully, the people of Luna would get the answers they deserved about the person responsible for this bomb, the closure that would help them move on with their lives.

Without it, they could try to move on. She'd

tried damn hard. She'd left behind everyone in her life and moved across the country, given up the job she'd dreamed of as a detective to become the police chief in a sleepy little town where she might spend six months of the year snowed in.

But she'd never actually found the peace she'd desperately searched for, the peace she'd almost convinced herself she'd achieved. Not if the sight of one smeared bloodstain could bring it all rushing back like this.

She'd never found her own closure. Not with her husband's killer still out there somewhere.

Chapter Two

Desparre's police chief walked away from him at a pace that looked purposeful, rather than desperate, the stomp of her boots echoing behind her.

Jax stared after her, intrigued. Even dressed down, she looked like someone who was used to being in charge. The dark hair she'd pulled back into a severe bun highlighted the sharp lines of her face, the thick eyebrows and exaggerated Cupid's bow of her lips. She looked like she had Mediterranean heritage, with perhaps a hint of Irish. It was hard to downplay beauty like hers, but she was obviously trying, with little to no makeup. Probably an attempt to get people to take her seriously. Women in law enforcement were the minority; women in high-level law-enforcement jobs even more so.

She was young for a police chief, although a place like Desparre probably didn't get a lot of crime. It was the sort of town where people came to disappear. Usually, those people weren't dangerous. They were running from a tragedy in their lives or from someone who meant them harm. Hiding out in the vast Alaskan wilderness, in somewhere like Desparre, which rarely rated mention on a map, would be a good option.

Keara probably didn't see much crime of

this scale. When a tiny town like Desparre—or Luna—faced a threat, they often didn't have the resources to handle it. Their police forces were small, too; their training often less than ideal.

But Alaska could be tough. With the constant threat of natural dangers, like blizzards or avalanches, frostbite or even wild animals, the people here learned to get tough, too, or get out, Jax had discovered.

Until six months ago Jax had lived in DC, working on the FBI's Rapid Deployment Team. Victim Specialists on that team worked a three-year term responding to mass casualties all over the country. When his time was up, Jax had been more than burnt out. Working as a private therapist for trauma victims had been intense in its own way, but it couldn't compare to the sheer volume of victims he could see in a single day, at a single site, with the FBI.

Moving to the Anchorage field office had felt like his chance to slow down. A chance to relax in Alaska's wild open spaces instead of DC's city center. He'd just finished training the puppy he'd found abandoned and scared, teaching her to work with victims. Coming to Alaska had felt like the right time to get her started as an official FBI dog.

He was the first Victim Specialist in the Anchorage office. Although they'd been unsure what to do with him initially, that had changed fast, putting him and Patches in high demand. Still, he hadn't been to any mass casualty events in Alaska until today.

Shaking off his exhaustion, Jax turned away from Keara Hernandez's retreating form as two agents jogged his way.

Ben Nez was a couple of years older than Jax's thirty-eight, with years of experience working in Alaska, since he'd spent most of his FBI career here—and before that, a good chunk of his life. His partner, Anderson Lync, was four years younger than Jax, and the office's designated "FNG." As Ben had explained it the first time Jax heard the term, Anderson was the "effing new guy." Because even though Anderson had been at Anchorage six months longer than Jax, they only gave agents the FNG designation, not mere Victim Specialists.

"We've got seven dead," Ben announced without preamble.

Anderson knelt down and pet Patches, probably as much to comfort himself as to be friendly. The younger agent looked worn out, his normally perfectly styled blond hair sticking up, exhaustion leaving half-moons under his eyes.

"Six died at the scene, one more at the hospital," Ben continued, speaking rapid-fire like he'd been mainlining coffee all day.

Or maybe after more than a decade with the Bureau, an agent just gained the ability to set aside the horror and exhaustion and be fueled simply by the desire to find those responsible. Whether it was getting numb after seeing a huge volume of tragedy or knowing from experience that pushing through was the only way to find answers, Jax wasn't sure.

"Twelve others are being treated in the hospital, and some are critical. Given the location choice..." Ben paused to gesture around them meaningfully, and Jax realized how serene this park must have been before the bomb. "We're probably looking at an intended target—or maybe targets—rather than someone trying to create fear or make some kind of statement. We'll need to get a lot deeper in this investigation to be sure, though. What have you heard from the victims, Jax?"

"Not much about a possible motive." Besides Akna and her mom, he'd spoken to a pair of locals who'd come by to see for themselves if it was really true, the parents of a victim who'd already been transported to the hospital and a handful of people who'd been near the park when the bomb exploded. Then he'd fielded calls from various family members asking for updates on the case's progress and collected as many details as he could about the victims so he could follow up with them personally. "So far all I'm hearing is shock. No mention of anyone with enemies. But right now my focus is getting them help."

"What about the soccer game?" Ben asked, not sounding surprised.

Normally, when Jax got called to a scene, he'd go with the investigators to interview victims, not do it himself. But often information came out when victims or family members were talking to Jax about details they didn't think were important or had forgotten to mention to the agents. Sometimes, it was one of those small details that led them to the perpetrator.

"It was posted on some kind of online community board." Jax repeated what Akna had told him. "Sounds pretty last-minute, but we can pull it up and check the time stamp."

"I already did," Anderson said, standing up, while Patches scooted over to Ben, and the veteran agent took his turn petting her.

What most agents didn't realize was that while the therapy dogs were there for the victims, they helped the investigators cope, too.

Anderson pulled out his phone and scrolled through notes, his lips moving silently until he finally said, "Eight a.m. About half an hour before the game started and an hour before the bomb went off."

"Not much time for someone to plant it if they were targeting one of the players," Ben mused. "Not to mention that not everyone who responded used their real names. Some of them are just screen names. Unfortunately, the guy who posted the idea about the game, Aiden DeMarco, died at the scene."

"But not all of the players were killed," Anderson said. "Maybe the bomber was going after one of the other people at the park. Or even someone who was supposed to be here, but left once they saw a game in progress."

Ben nodded slowly. "Or they'd been targeting one of the soccer players and they planted it quickly when they learned that person would be here this morning. That game drastically increased the number of people who were hurt or killed today."

"Was the bomb on a timer?" Jax asked. "Or did someone set it off remotely?"

"Looks like it was set off remotely," Ben replied. "Probably with a cell phone, but we'll know more after the lab techs get their hands on it. We sent it to the lab six hours ago. Hopefully, we'll have the answer tomorrow. In the meantime..." He stared meaningfully at Jax.

"You want me to come with you to the hospital? See if any of the victims saw anything?"

"The fresher it is in their minds, usually the better," Anderson said.

"No problem," Jax agreed, even though he knew that was only partially true. Sure, memories faded over time. But with trauma, the mind could block out pieces. Sometimes, those details only returned later.

He gave Patches an encouraging smile. "Want to go help some more people?"

Woof!

Ben jerked slightly at Patches's enthusiastic reply, but Anderson just smiled. "She handles this part of it better than any of us."

"Kind of," Jax replied, but Ben and Anderson were already heading toward the SUV.

The truth was, dogs were susceptible to depression from this kind of work, too. They needed breaks, just like people did. But there was no denying that Patches loved cheering people up. Right now she was staring at him expectantly, then glancing toward the SUV, knowing she had more work to do.

He smiled at her, then lifted his arm, directing it toward the vehicle. "Okay, Patches, let's go."

The hospital was going to be his next stop anyway. He ignored the growl of his stomach reminding him he hadn't eaten anything since the quick sandwich he'd grabbed four hours ago. He had hours left before his day would be over.

Hopefully, one of the victims at the hospital would have answers that would get them closer to the bomber. Because if Anderson was right and the intended target of the bomb hadn't been on scene, would the bomber try again?

AFTER SEVEN LONG years alone, the memories shouldn't have been so close to the surface.

Keara stared into the whiskey she'd ordered hours ago, but had barely touched. The amber liquid reflected back a distorted version of the hand under her chin, a hand that had once worn a thin gold band, no diamond to get in the way on the job.

She hadn't had such a vivid flashback to Juan's murder in years. The bomb scene was nothing like her husband's murder. The thick jagged slice across her husband's neck, the blood pooled underneath him, the crickets chirping happily in the background. Her scream echoing through the tiny yard, making a neighbor call the police, because she was too traumatized to move. Too shocked to do her own job because she'd known with a single look that he was already gone. And she'd never even suspected there was a threat.

When the investigation began, she'd been told repeatedly to stay out of it. It was her husband, but it wasn't her case. She'd understood that, believed in her fellow detectives, believed Juan would get justice. But a year later the case had gone cold, the detectives insisting they'd done all they could, that they'd loved him, too. In that moment she'd known she couldn't stay. Not with the Houston PD, not in the life she and Juan had built together. Not if she wanted to be able to move forward.

It's over, Keara reminded herself, squeezing the whiskey glass but not lifting it to her lips. She'd made her choice when she moved to Alaska. Let go or drown in it. Those had been her options six years ago and she'd picked *let go*.

At least she thought she had.

Except here she was, failing to do her job because of the past. Pushing the whiskey away from her, Keara glanced around the old-fashioned bar on the outskirts of Luna. Between the claustrophobic closeness of the booths jammed together and the heater turned up to battle the chill that slid underneath the ill-fitting door, the air was stuffy and beer-scented. She'd chosen it because she'd wanted to be alone in a room full of people, rather than truly alone in her vehicle and then her house.

Although it was nearly twice the size of tiny Desparre—in terms of population, if not geography—there weren't many options late at night in Luna. She'd hoped a quiet booth and a short glass of whiskey would calm her nerves. Instead, she'd choked on the only sip of whiskey she'd taken. And there was nothing quiet about this bar.

Since moving to Alaska, she'd become a loner. It was a trait many of her citizens shared, for myriad reasons. For her, it was partly because of her job. A chief of police didn't fraternize with colleagues or civilians too much. Especially not a female chief of police who was new to Alaska and wanted to be taken seriously.

The rest of it, of course, was Juan. Although peo-

ple in Desparre usually let you keep your secrets—
because they often had their own they didn't want
to open up about—real friendship dictated honesty. After living here for six years, Keara still
wasn't sure if she was ready for honesty.

Now she glanced around the bar, wondering if
all the small decisions she'd made to isolate herself had brought her right back to where she'd
started. Sinking into grief.

She needed to go home. But there was something vaguely calming about having people
around her, people she didn't know, who mostly
left her alone. The bar was closer to Luna's lone
hotel than it was to downtown. She didn't recognize anyone, and the snippets of conversation
that reached her said most of these people were
outsiders.

There was a group of guys in jeans and T-shirts
who'd been drinking since before she'd walked
through the door and already hit on her more than
once. A loner at the bar drinking soda water and
eyeing the hard stuff. And a couple at the other
end of the bar who'd jammed their stools as close
together as possible while they flirted. She'd bet a
week's pay that none of them had been in Alaska
longer than a few days.

Still, they weren't immune to what was happening here. In between lewd jokes from the
group of drinkers, the alcohol-tainted conversation beside her would shift to the bombing.

"I heard a couple more died in the hospital."

"No one else died, man. But I think one of them had to have a leg amputated because it was blown mostly off in the explosion."

"Someone was trying to kill one of those soccer players."

"Nah, this is terrorism. You'll see. They'll start hitting bigger parks next, take out more people."

Only the two men hunkered down near the door sharing a couple of pints looked like locals. One of them periodically patted his friend's shoulder awkwardly and glared at the out-of-towners. The guy getting the sympathy had red-rimmed eyes, ruddy cheeks and a knocked-over pile of shot glasses beside him.

She'd recognized the look as soon as she walked into the bar and chosen a seat on the opposite end of the place. Against the wall, where she could see everyone, but she tried to avoid glancing their way. One of them had lost someone they loved tonight. Keara couldn't bear to hear about it.

She dragged her gaze away from him and tried to focus on what she needed to do next. It was after eleven, well past the time when the Luna Police Department shut down for the night. But after the bombing—even with the FBI on the case—maybe someone would still be there. She could stop by on her way home, hopefully get some real answers she could share with her officers, with her town.

Setting aside her whiskey, Keara stood. She wasn't ready to face the drive up and down the mountain, or the emptiness of her house that she knew would feel more lonely than usual tonight. But she was still the chief of police. And she had people who needed answers.

"Hey, at least there's only six dead," one of the guys at the rowdy table slurred. "Could have been way worse."

Before Keara could maneuver free of her booth, the big guy who'd lost someone he loved was up and screaming.

Then he was diving across the small bar, leading with fists and grief. His punch landed, sending the guy who'd spoken to the floor. Then the guy's friends jumped on his attacker, and suddenly, everyone seemed to be in the fray. Even the loner at the counter grabbed an abandoned beer bottle off the bar and chucked it. The way he swayed violently when he did it told her that although he'd been drinking soda water since she'd arrived, he'd imbibed plenty of alcohol beforehand.

Only the couple near the door leaped up and ran out of the bar, away from the fight.

The bartender reached under the counter and Keara knew what was coming. She tried to get ahead of it, holding up her badge and screaming, "Police. Stop!"

But the bartender was quick, yanking his shotgun up and over the top of the bar, racking it loudly.

Keara heard it and flinched, but no one else paid any attention, not even when the bartender yelled, "Stop it or I'll shoot!"

"Sir, put the shotgun away!" Keara yelled at him, but the bar had gotten louder.

One of the men in the group closest to her spotted her badge and yelled, "Cop!"

Then the group was shifting, a furious mob coming for her fast.

She backed up, trying to protect her weapon as she pulled out her mace and sprayed it across the group. The noxious fumes spilled back toward her, clogging her throat and making her eyes water.

The group kept coming, too drunk or unthinking.

Keara backed up another step, but then her back slammed into something protruding from the wall and there was nowhere left to go. The four men who'd been hitting on her were rushing her from one direction. The two men who'd been grieving got in the mix, too, still going for the drunken group.

She was about to get overrun by them all.

Chapter Three

Twelve hospital rooms, filled with pain and fear and disbelief. Twelve victims, trying to recover from burns and deep cuts and in one case, an amputation. Twelve families, furious and scared and feeling helpless.

Jax and Patches had visited them all this evening. Some as briefly as five minutes, when the victims or the family didn't have the energy or inclination to talk to the FBI. Others as long as half an hour, the longest the agents would allow since they wanted to talk to everyone before the night ended.

Jax glanced at the base of his bed back at his hotel, where Patches had the right idea. Her tongue lolled slightly out of her mouth, her feet periodically twitching in her sleep. As soon as they'd returned to the hotel, she'd hopped up into bed and fallen fast asleep.

He needed to do the same. But despite being emotionally worn out, he was still hungry, since he hadn't ever found time for dinner. Part of him was still amped up, feeling the pressure from all directions. A need to help the victims and families move forward. A need to help the investigators get information to find the person responsible.

Slipping quietly out of the hotel room, he slid on his coat and trudged down the stairs. The hotel didn't have its own restaurant, and as far as he could tell, the only thing nearby that was open was a bar. He didn't want a drink, but maybe they'd have food. At this point he'd settle for peanuts.

He zipped his coat up to his chin and huddled low in it. Springtime in Alaska was beautiful, but it wasn't warm.

On his way out, he waved to Ben and Anderson, who were still slumped in the lobby chairs, trading case notes.

"Where to?" Ben asked, raising an eyebrow when Jax answered, "Bar down the road."

Jax looked them over, in the same spot he'd left them after they'd returned from the hospital. "Did you two ever eat dinner?"

"Power bars," Anderson said. Without looking up from his phone, he tossed one to Jax. "I always travel with them."

"Thanks." The protein-heavy power bar was probably better than anything he'd get in the bar, and Jax hesitated, debating returning to his room. But he was too antsy to sleep and although he liked Ben and Anderson, he needed a break from the case. "See you later."

When he stepped through the door out into the frigid Alaskan air, Jax knew it was what he needed. A walk probably would have been better than the bar, but he didn't know the area and he didn't want to get lost or run into a wild animal. So instead, he walked quickly toward the log-cabin-style establishment. The walk was long enough to make his nose and ears sting from the cold, but not long enough to clear his head.

He heard it when he was fifteen feet away. Yelling and crashing sounds. Probably a fight, definitely too many people involved.

Then a couple holding hands darted out of the bar and ran toward him.

"What's happening?" he asked.

"People are mad and drinking," the woman said, only pausing briefly as they continued past him, toward the hotel. "It turned into a big fight. I wouldn't go in there."

Yanking out his cell phone, he texted Ben and Anderson a message.

Bar fight. Call the Luna police? Or earn your community badges today...

A bar fight was a local PD problem, not the purview of the FBI. But the agents were close and Luna police had a lot to manage right now. Jax didn't know which option Ben and Anderson would choose. But he figured doubling up couldn't hurt. He'd just started to dial the Luna police chief directly when a female voice cut through the yelling. A voice he recognized, slightly husky and naturally commanding. But right now underlaid with definite panic.

Dropping his phone into his pocket, Jax raced inside.

Five angry and obviously drunk men were crowded near the side wall, some of them holding beer bottles aloft like weapons. All of them were yelling, most of it incoherent, but what Jax could make out were a mix of violent threats and juvenile insults. Two were facing off against each other, shifting back and forth, glowering.

A sixth was passed out half on a table, half on the floor, and looked like he needed stitches. A seventh stood near the bar, holding his own beer bottle and watching the spectacle with a wide grin. The bartender stood behind him, brandishing a shotgun but looking uncertain.

Where was Keara?

Jax strained to see, then realized. She was behind the pack of men, ordering them to back up. From the way his eyes started watering and his throat was suddenly on fire as he took one step farther inside and the door slammed shut behind him, he realized she'd sprayed them with mace. It seemed to have only made them angrier.

Fear tightened his chest, knowing she was trapped behind the angry group. Could he wade into them, give Keara a chance to slide free?

He rejected the idea immediately. There were too many of them, fueled by alcohol and fury, likely to take any physical contact as an invitation to resume fighting.

Still, he had to do something. The two who'd been circling each other had turned toward Keara, and from the way they shared a sudden look of agreement, they were about to rush her.

Jax wasn't armed. Even if he was, it probably wouldn't help, based on the bartender's worried shake of his head.

"I already called the police," the bartender yelled at him. "If I fire this now, it might go through those guys and hit the lady back there. She's in trouble."

Jax swore and looked around for something he could use as a weapon, even though he knew it was useless. What he needed was Ben and Anderson, a way to even the numbers.

Leaping on top of the bar, Jax bellowed, "FBI!"

As one, the group turned toward him, but they only lowered their fists and bottles for a split second. Then they were up again, and the group was turning back toward each other.

Faster than he would have thought possible, while the men were distracted, Keara slid along the wall, breaking free of the group. She had her pistol out and leveled at the man who seemed to be the primary instigator.

"I'm chief of police in Desparre!" she yelled. "And the man on the bar is with the FBI. Put the bottles down and back away right now!"

For a moment it seemed like it might work.

Then the big guy in front swayed a little and yelled back, "You can't get us all, bi—"

"People died today!" Jax cut him off as Keara took a slow step backward, closer to him.

They froze, their attention redirecting his way. "We're searching for a *bomber* right now! You really want to end up in jail for threatening a police chief?"

Two of the men shook their heads, set down their bottles and stepped away from the group, holding up their hands.

Two of the others hesitated, their bottles lowering slightly.

But the big guy in front flushed an even deeper, patchy red and announced, "You're not FBI! You're not even armed!"

A flash of movement below Jax caught his attention. Too fast for Jax to move out of the way, the loner who'd been watching with glee grabbed hold of his leg and yanked hard.

Jax flung out his arms, trying to brace himself, hoping his head wouldn't smack the top of the bar as he crashed downward, sliding awkwardly, painfully, off it. Broken glass sliced through his arms, and his back scraped the edge of the bar as his legs slammed into the bar stools, knocking them over.

Then he was on the ground, trying to catch his

breath and focus through the pain in his head, and a bottle was crashing toward his face.

Knowing it wouldn't be fast enough, he tried to roll away.

The guy over him suddenly stiffened, his eyes going unnaturally wide. Then he toppled over, the bottle crashing down inches from Jax's face and luckily not shattering.

Behind him, Keara had her gun trained on the group who'd frozen again, and her other arm directed his way, wires extending from the Taser in her hand to the guy on the ground beside him, still stiff and moaning.

Then the door burst open and Ben and Anderson were there, weapons out, yelling, "FBI!"

As they rushed into the room, giving Keara an approving nod, Ben glanced down at him with a mix of concern and amusement.

"You've got to stop playing agent, Jax."

SHE'D GOTTEN LUCKY.

Although no officer was immune to the danger of being caught alone and outnumbered, at least in Houston, backup tended to be relatively close. You might get caught in a dangerous situation—and it wasn't uncommon—but you'd probably be in the thick of it with other officers. In Alaska, the danger was far less persistent. But you were way more likely to be caught alone. The distance it could take the closest officer to come to your aid could be deadly even if you held off the threat for a long time.

Keara had been reaching the end of that time when Jax had walked into the bar.

She glanced at him now, sitting across from her on a couch in the lobby of the hotel down the street from the bar. He was grimacing in a T-shirt, his bloodied sweater in a bundle next to him along with his coat, as one of the agents—a tall, lean blond guy who'd introduced himself as Anderson—wrapped his arms with gauze.

"There's no glass left behind," Anderson said. "I was SWAT for a while in DC, so I had to get some basic medical training, but you still might want to go back to the hospital. Most of these cuts will close up, but this one—" he pointed at the last, deepest cut he'd bandaged "—might scar unless you get it stitched."

"I'm fine," Jax said tightly.

"Yeah, I get it. I wouldn't want to go back there, either," Anderson said. "That was a rough evening, talking to all those victims. Especially the one who lost her leg, whose fiancé died in the blast. I don't know how—"

"You should have stayed outside," Ben cut his partner off. "You keep forgetting—you're not an agent." He glanced at Keara, eyes narrowing as he studied her. "Was this all drunken, overemotional idiocy or did you hear anything we might want to know for our investigation?"

She didn't have to glance at Jax to feel his embarrassment, but the truth was, she'd needed him tonight. Law enforcement or not, his presence—and presence of mind—had definitely saved her from getting hurt. Maybe even from getting killed.

"Idiocy," she confirmed, trying not to cringe as she subtly probed her lower back with her fingers. Between the time she'd maced the group and Jax had arrived, she'd been shoved into the wall, right where some kind of decoration hung. The bruise ached with every quick movement.

"And grief," she added, remembering the man who'd burst into tears when Luna police arrived and cuffed the whole lot to escort them to cells. His younger sister had died in the explosion.

Her hand shook as she stopped pushing on the bruise and it wasn't all from pain. The bruise was nasty, but she didn't need medical care, just time to heal. It was also adrenaline, still pumping as if she hadn't left that bar. As if she hadn't gotten away from the crowd of men towering over her with bottles and fists and anger they were willing to redirect at the nearest available target. Especially one who'd just sprayed them all with mace.

With six years on the police force in a big city like Houston—five of them on patrol—Keara had faced plenty of dicey situations. Most of them with a partner at her back, but a few alone. Back then she'd lived with a different level of awareness at all times.

In Alaska, she'd gotten used to needing to be wary of the elements more often than the people. She should have positioned herself near the door. Should have ignored her emotional desire to avoid the grief-stricken man there and picked a spot near the exit. She still might have been overrun, but she probably could have gotten to a safe distance to pull her weapon sooner. Maybe stopped the brawl faster, without anyone getting hurt.

"So Keara," Ben said as Anderson finished patching up Jax, "you were at the scene a few hours ago."

When he stared at her assessingly, as if waiting for her to confirm what he already knew, she nodded.

"Did you notice anything unusual? Anyone hanging around who seemed off?"

Ben didn't need to clarify as all three of them stared at her, waiting for an answer.

At the scene of a bombing, in a small town full of people who liked their business to be their business, it would be easy to slip into the edges of a group. Pretend to be sympathizing. Pretend to be there out of safety concerns or empathy for neighbors, while actually reveling in your handiwork.

Police officers—especially someone like her, who'd spent years on patrol in a busy city—

learned to spot the outliers. People who were trying to blend in, but were just a little too focused. On the woman alone, walking in front of them. Or the fire blazing in a building, origins unknown. Or the devastation of an attack, like a bombing.

Keara mentally reviewed the people she'd noticed at the edges of the scene, near the hastily assembled memorial made of candles and flowers and stuffed animals, or down the street, pointing and shaking their heads. Everyone had looked the way she'd felt. Shocked. Horrified. Like a veneer of safety had just been ripped away, revealing a vulnerability they'd never expected.

She shook her head. "I don't think so. I don't know everyone here. Not even close. But many of the people on scene I recognized at least vaguely. If the bomber was there, he's a good actor."

"Or she," Anderson put in.

Keara shrugged, acknowledging that truth, although as far as she knew, bombers were more likely to be male. Running murder investigations in Houston had told her that men liked to kill violently: strangulation, bullet wounds, stabbing. Women were less likely to murder in the first place, but more likely to use arson or poison. And they were more likely to kill a single person; men were significantly more likely to kill multiples or commit mass murders. Of course, those were generalizations. Bombings weren't something she'd ever investigated.

"What about this?" Ben asked, sounding like he already expected the answer to be negative. "This is a bomb fragment. Does the symbol on it look familiar? Does it mean anything to you?" He held out his phone, zoomed in so she could see the detail, the series of interconnecting loops.

Distantly, she felt Jax leap up and grab her arm as she swayed. She heard Anderson's surprised "You know it?"

But she couldn't focus enough to answer. The lobby around her spun in dizzying circles as her whole body seemed to catch fire and her lungs couldn't get enough oxygen.

She'd seen that symbol once before, seven years ago. On the wall at a murder scene in one of Juan's last investigations before he was killed.

Chapter Four

Could their bomber be connected to a case Keara's husband had investigated seven years ago?

Jax's heart thudded too hard as he watched Keara, her olive-toned skin too pale, a sudden tightness around her eyes and mouth. The knowledge that she was a widow surprised him, filled him with sadness for what she'd experienced, along with a tinge of jealousy. Ridiculous and inappropriate, but he was self-aware enough to recognize why. He'd been instantly intrigued by her, attracted to her. Seeing her in trouble in the bar, then seeing her in action, had only increased those feelings.

None of that mattered. Not when she was staring back at them, trying to get it together after she'd announced that her dead husband had investigated a case with the same symbol. Not when she might have the key to the investigation.

Ben and Anderson were staring at her, too. Ben's fingers tapped a frantic beat against his chair and Anderson was leaning toward her, hanging half out of his seat. But both of them were experienced enough not to rush her.

Finally, her fingers loosened the death grip they'd had on the couch since he'd helped her sit. "I haven't seen that symbol in seven years."

"Are you sure it's the same symbol?" Ben asked.

She held out her hand for his phone, then zoomed in and stared at it a long moment. "I'm pretty sure. It might not be exact, but it's close enough to look connected."

"Tell us about this case," Anderson requested.

"It was a murder," she said and some of the intense energy radiating from Ben and Anderson instantly deflated.

Jax had been part of enough investigations—even though he was on the periphery—to know why. A murder was pretty different from a bombing.

"The victim, Celia Harris, was fairly well-known in Houston. She owned a popular chain of bakeries and was always volunteering her time to local charity events. The press picked up news of her murder fast, maybe because she had two young kids and was killed in a back alley in a bad part of town. Probably also because the murder was violent. That symbol was spray-painted on the wall behind her. I didn't work the case, but I know Juan and his partner suspected it was going to be the start of a series of killings."

"They thought it was a serial killer?" Ben asked. "Why?"

"None of the obvious suspects panned out. There were signs Celia had been abducted and probably not by someone she knew. They thought the symbol was a serial killer's signature."

Anderson scooted back in his seat, looking less anxious the more Keara spoke. "But..."

"But there were no more killings that matched. They never saw the symbol again. Well, Juan's partner didn't. Juan died a few weeks into the investigation."

Jax didn't ask the question he most wanted to know the answer to right now: What had happened to her husband?

Instead, he glanced from Ben to Anderson. He knew them well enough to recognize their waning interest. They didn't think this was connected. But the symbol was unusual, an odd series of interconnecting loops that he'd heard the agents say earlier didn't mean anything they could identify.

"Any idea what the symbol means?" Jax asked Keara.

She shrugged. "Juan and his partner thought it was the killer's own design."

"How sure were they that the killer actually drew the symbol? Couldn't it have been spray-painted before the murder happened?"

Keara shrugged, suddenly looking exhausted. "I didn't ask for particulars. I just knew they'd determined it was put there by the killer. You can contact the Houston PD for more details. Juan's partner is still there, as far as I know. I don't keep in close touch with the department, but I don't think the murder was ever solved."

Ben nodded and Anderson wrote down the contact information for Juan's partner, but Jax didn't need to ask to know it was low on their list of priorities. They'd follow up—they were both good agents—but despite the strange symbol, they didn't think it was connected. And he understood why. The symbol was too generic, the crimes too different. Besides, there were too many variables. They couldn't even be sure the murderer in Keara's husband's case had been the one to draw the symbol. Alleyways were often filled with random graffiti, especially in a big city like Houston.

Keara stood, flinching in a way that told him that he wasn't the only one who'd left that bar with injuries. The closed-off expression on her face said she wouldn't welcome him asking about it, so instead he asked, "Are you okay to drive home? Desparre isn't exactly close."

"Out here, it's about as close as you get," she replied, her chin tilting up just slightly. "Thanks for the help," she added, her gaze sweeping the three of them, lingering briefly on him before she headed for the door.

"The symbol is unusual," Jax said once she'd left the hotel and it was just him and the agents in the brightly lit lobby.

"It's not connected," Ben said, rubbing a hand across his eyes.

"I'll call the partner and follow up anyway,"

Anderson added, "but Ben is right. It's strange, but coincidences happen."

"I don't know—"

"Jax, you want to talk to her about this more? Be my guest," Ben said, glancing at his watch and standing. "But you know as well as we do that it's unlikely there's a solid link here. Yeah, the symbol is odd, but it's not particularly unique. And we can't even be sure the killer in her husband's case is the one who drew it. She said it was spray-painted on an alley wall. Could have been some random tagger practicing. Our symbol was literally on the bomb fragment. That's pretty different."

"Maybe, but—"

"An alley in downtown Houston at a murder site. And a bomb fragment in the middle of nowhere, Alaska. A single murder and a bombing that's already killed seven and injured at least twelve more. You've got the psychology background, so you tell me: How likely is it that a violent murderer turned into a bomber?"

"Not very," Jax agreed, trying not to be distracted by the way his arms stung, the way his back and legs and head throbbed. The two aspirin he'd gotten from the hotel desk hadn't done much to ease the pain.

From the type of murder Keara had described, the killer had wanted to get up close. He thrived on the brutality, on causing someone else to suffer, on watching that suffering up close and personal. He'd probably loved the attention, the big press coverage in a big city. A bomber was a different personality type. Someone who *didn't* want to be hands-on for the actual kill. Someone who wanted to see more destruction, but choosing a place so far off the map meant maybe he wasn't looking for the intensity of news coverage.

"Still…"

"What?" Anderson prompted when Jax went silent.

Jax's specialty was working with trauma victims, helping them reclaim control over their emotions and their lives. He'd spent time analyzing the motives behind the perpetrators, but only if it was in service of the survivors.

But the more time he'd spent working for the FBI, the more he'd realized that the specialty translated. And not just as a Victim Specialist, but also in providing real insight into the way the perpetrators thought.

He didn't know enough about the case Keara's husband had investigated to be able to say if it was connected or not. But something about it kept nudging his brain.

"The symbol was on the bomb fragment," Jax said. "That means it's important. But maybe the bomber didn't expect it to survive the blast. Maybe he drew it for himself."

"Maybe," Ben agreed.

"So maybe he never expected it to be connected to a seven-year-old murder."

"IS THERE ANY news on the Luna bombing?" Tate Emory, an officer she'd brought on to the Desparre PD just over five years ago, leaned his head into her office.

Tate was one of her most easygoing officers, with a calm under pressure none of her veterans had expected. Of course, they only knew Tate's cover story, believed he'd been a true rookie when he joined the force. But Keara knew he'd been a police officer before hiding away in this remote Alaskan town. Because she'd kept his secret, he was one of the only people here who knew anything about her past.

Still, she wasn't about to share the possible connection to one of her husband's cases. Not when the FBI had grown less and less interested the longer she'd spoken. Not when the light of day was bringing her own doubts.

Last night she'd been so certain. This morning, back at work in Desparre and fielding calls from concerned citizens about their neighboring town, she wondered if she was wrong.

It had been seven years since she'd seen that symbol. Yes, years on the force had enhanced her skills of observation and memory. But maybe it wasn't the same. Even she had to admit it didn't look like much beyond doodling. Or maybe both a murderer and a bomber had seen the same symbol somewhere and used it themselves.

"The FBI is managing the investigation." She told Tate what he'd surely already seen on the news. "I couldn't get anything useful out of them."

An image of Jax, crashing down from the top of that bar after he'd tried to help her, filled her mind. There was something compelling about him. And it was more than the tall, dark and handsome thing he had going for him, or the adorable dog who followed him around.

It was the eyes, she realized. The way they'd fixed on her, given her one hundred percent of his attention. A psychologist's trick, surely, but it had felt personal.

"They have no suspects?"

Keara shook off thoughts of Jax and focused on Tate. The officer was only a few years younger than her own thirty-five, but the way he carried himself made him seem like he'd seen a lot over those years.

"If they do, they didn't share the details with me." She thought about the exhaustion on the two agents' faces in the lobby of the Luna hotel last night, going over evidence after a full day at a bomb site. "I think they're struggling to figure out a motive."

"That was a big blast. Seems like it was someone who had experience making bombs," Tate said. "Then again, these days any criminal-minded sociopath can find a recipe to make a bomb on the internet."

Keara nodded, her gaze moving to the open door of her office. Resisting the urge to ask him if he'd dealt with bombings in his previous job, she said, "I got cards from several FBI agents and their Victim Specialist. I'll stay in contact."

"Sounds good."

As Tate turned back for the bullpen, Keara said, "Close the door behind you, please."

Once she was alone, she dialed a number she hadn't called since she'd moved to Alaska. For all she knew, he'd changed it. A small part of her—the part that really did want to leave the past behind her—hoped he had changed it.

"Fitz," he answered on the first ring, his voice a deep grumble created by years of smoking and drinking.

The familiar voice instantly took her back to the swampy summers in Houston, to responding to a dangerous call one last time with Juan before he took the promotion to detective and partnered up with veteran Leroy Fitzgerald. Leaving her to work with a rookie for a year, before she made the jump to detective herself. But by then, they were engaged and rules prohibited them from working together anymore.

"You talk or I hang up," Fitz snapped.

"It's Keara Hernandez," she blurted, relieved when her voice sounded only slightly strained.

She and Fitz had never gotten along. She'd tolerated him because he was Juan's partner and a partner's trust on the force could be the difference between life and death. He'd tolerated her for the same reason.

"Keara."

His voice softened in a way she'd only come to know after Juan had died, when Fitz had been sidelined like her, and two other detectives were assigned to investigate. Unlike her, Fitz had been allowed to stay close to the investigation, even tag along at the end.

"How's Alaska?"

His voice was neutral, but she'd always suspected he was glad when she left Houston. When she stopped hassling him and everyone else for details on her husband's case. When she'd stopped making all of them feel guilty for failing, no matter how hard they'd tried. She'd been the final holdout, the last person to accept the case would never be solved.

If the sudden pain burning its way up her chest was any indication, she'd never truly accepted it. She'd only run from it.

"Peaceful, mostly." She got right to business, not wanting to hear about life on the force she'd left behind—assuming he was still on the force. "I'm calling because there's a case up here with a symbol that I think matches the one from that murder you and Juan caught at the end. The one you thought was a serial?" She was purposely vague about the Alaskan case, phrasing it in a way that wouldn't be lying if she had to admit it wasn't her case at all, but hopefully not inviting questions.

"Really?" He sounded surprised, but only vaguely interested. "Another murder?"

"Not exactly. Could you fax me the details? I want to see if my memory is as good as I think it is. See if the symbol really is the same."

There was a pause long enough to make Keara silently swear, before Fitz asked slowly, "I'm guessing since you called me on my personal line that this is an unofficial request?"

"Yes."

"Is this about Juan?"

The pain that had been creeping up her chest clamped down hard. "Why? What do you mean?"

"Nothing. I just… I figured if I ever heard from you again, it would be because you'd finally started investigating Juan's death on your own." He let out a forced laugh. "You always were dogged. Kind of a rule-breaker."

It was a much more polite version of what she'd overheard some of her colleagues in Texas saying about her when she'd been a patrol officer, even after she'd become a detective. They were traits she'd tried hard to tame when she'd come to Alaska.

Follow the rules, for the most part. Definitely not date anyone within her ranks. She'd barely befriended them, determined to keep her distance. Not just to maintain her authority, but also to protect herself. Being a police officer was a dangerous profession, even in a quiet little town like Desparre. The officers here had become her responsibility and she took that seriously. If someone died on her watch, she needed to be able to stay removed enough to do what had to be done, to keep the rest of the team going.

Of course it was important to be persistent, to chase down the truth no matter what. But there was also value in learning when to let go.

It was something she thought she'd succeeded in.

"Is there some reason to think Celia Harris's murder was connected to Juan's death?" she asked tightly. If there was, they'd all kept it from her back then.

"No," Fitz replied.

"Are you sure?" she demanded, suddenly certain he was keeping something from her.

"Yeah, I'm sure. As sure as I can be. I mean, we don't know who the hell took Juan out. Just because Juan's case went cold six years ago doesn't mean we all gave up on it."

It was only the hurt underneath the anger in

Fitz's voice that kept Keara from snapping at him. When the case had officially gone cold, she'd done the only thing she could do to survive it. She'd tried to shut down that part of her life entirely, remove herself from any reminders that she'd ever been married, that she'd ever faced such a loss. And she'd done it in spectacular fashion, by running as far away as she could.

"Have you found anything?" she demanded, anger seeping into her own voice. Whatever Fitz thought of her decision to leave Houston, she was still Juan's wife. She still deserved answers.

"No."

In that single word, she heard all of the defeat she'd felt six years ago, when the chief had officially called off the active investigation, told the detectives on Juan's case they had to move on.

Closing her eyes, Keara let out a long breath, trying to regain her composure. "Tell me about Celia Harris's murder, then. Please. You never found any likely suspects, did you?"

"Well…"

Her eyes popped back open. "Who?"

"Your husband went to talk to someone whose car was near the scene of the murder. A hospital orderly with some minor criminal history named Rodney Brown."

A mix of dread and anger made her pulse speed up. "You remember the name all these years later? Why?"

"Juan talked to the guy on kind of a long-shot lead. I didn't go with him. He said it didn't look like anything, but that Rodney kept insisting the whole thing was a mistake. That he hadn't taken his car out at all. It struck Juan as a little weird, but he thought maybe Rodney was just nervous about being interviewed by a police officer. I wouldn't have thought anything of it, either, except Rodney disappeared a few weeks later."

Keara let the timeline sink in and her anger intensified. "A few weeks later. So you're telling me this guy disappeared right after Juan was killed?"

"We looked into it," Fitz insisted. "We couldn't find any evidence that he was involved in Juan's murder."

"You couldn't find any because it didn't look like he'd done it or because he disappeared and you couldn't find him?"

When Fitz didn't immediately respond, Keara jumped to her feet. Through the glass walls of her office, she saw some of her officers staring at her with curiosity and concern.

She turned her back on them, knowing there was no way she could hide the horror she felt. "You think it was him."

"I did," Fitz said quietly. "But no one else agreed, Keara. And seven years later I wonder if I was just reaching for anything. For anyone I could blame. He was my partner. It eats me up every day that we couldn't solve his murder."

"Why the hell didn't you tell me?"

"What would you have done?"

Investigated on her own. She would have done whatever it took to find Rodney Brown and figure out if he'd killed her husband.

"That's why I didn't tell you," Fitz said, without her saying a word. "Because we chased that lead as far as we could. It was a dead end. And…" He let out a heavy sigh. "You deserved to move on. Juan would have wanted that."

Keara grit her teeth, trying to hold back the tears suddenly threatening. "Just send me the file, Fitz."

She hung up before he could say anything else, then planted her hands on her credenza for stability. Seven years. Someone who might have killed Juan had had seven long years to run. Seven long years for the trail to go cold.

Was it possible he'd shown up here, stepped up the volume of his kills by becoming a bomber?

Chapter Five

"Does this symbol look familiar to you?" Jax held up the digitally enhanced image that had been found on a bomb fragment.

Gabi Sinclair winced as she hauled herself up higher against the headboard of the hospital bed. Her sheet slid downward and she immediately hiked it up, avoiding looking at the leg that had been amputated below the knee yesterday. Her light brown skin was tinged with an ashy gray, her eyes bloodshot.

When Jax had met her last night, she hadn't been able to stop crying about the fiancé who'd died in the blast. Today she was all gritted teeth and desperate determination, wanting any information she could get about the investigation. A mix of numbness and anger that would only last so long before the grief bled through again.

Hopefully, when that happened, he'd be able to help her.

She stared at the symbol intently for a long minute, her free hand dropping down beside the bed to pet Patches, who'd been patiently waiting. Finally, she shook her head. "I don't know it. What is it?"

From slightly behind him, Jax sensed Ben and Anderson's disappointment, heard their suit coats slumping against the rough hospital wall. They'd taken the lead today, but asked him along to make the victims and their families feel more comfortable. The more rooms they visited, the more questions Jax asked. Technically, it was the agents' job to ask about the symbol, but for some of the victims, he suspected it would be easier to talk to him.

Gabi was their final hospital visit. None of the victims they'd spoken to had recognized the symbol.

"This was drawn on one of the bomb fragments," Anderson spoke up, stepping forward in the tight space. "We don't know what it means. It might be nothing. But we're checking everything."

Gabi frowned slightly, directing her gaze at Patches, who scooted closer to the bed and made the tiniest smile quiver at the corner of Gabi's lips.

"When we have some answers, we'll tell you what we can," Jax said, not wanting to overpromise what he might not be able to deliver, but also wanting to help start the healing process. If Gabi felt like she was cut off from real information, it would only increase the helplessness she felt.

She nodded at him, her hand stalling against Patches's head, her brow furrowed like she was trying to puzzle it out, too.

Despite research done by Ben and Anderson—

and some curiosity searching Jax had done himself on publicly available sites—none of them understood it. They'd found symbols that were similar, but nothing close enough and so far, nothing else tied to a crime like this. If the bomber had been trying to send a message with the symbol, it appeared to be one only he understood.

Maybe the case Keara's husband had investigated would provide the break they needed. When Jax had pressed him on it that morning, Anderson said he was waiting for a call back from the Houston detective.

"Is there anything else you can remember from yesterday morning?" Ben asked, stepping up next to Jax, crowding him just slightly, like he wanted Jax to step back.

Gabi glanced from him to Ben, then shook her head. "Not really. Carter and I were just going for a walk." Her voice trembled on her fiancé's name, then she cleared her throat and kept going. "We'd stopped to sit on the bench for a few minutes when it happened."

"And you didn't notice anyone behaving strangely?" Ben asked. "No one leaving the park or staring at it from a distance?"

The FBI had gotten news back from the lab that morning that the bomb had been set off remotely. That made it more likely the bomber had been nearby, watching for the exact moment he wanted it to detonate.

Gabi shook her head quickly, but she'd answered these questions before.

"Thanks, Gabi," Jax said. "I know this isn't easy. But if you think of anything—even if you're not sure it matters—you can call any of us. And if you need to talk, I'm just a phone call away, day or night. You know Patches is always excited to come and see you."

Beside her bed, Patches let out an affirmative *woof!*

Gabi startled at the sudden noise, then gave his dog a tiny smile.

Anderson shot him a look, but Jax ignored it. Technically, telling a victim they could call in the middle of the night was dangerous territory. He'd known Victim Specialists who'd fallen into roles halfway between personal therapist and best friend by being too available. But he worried more about not helping enough than being overwhelmed by a victim's needs.

As Jax and Patches started to follow the agents out of the room, Gabi's voice, more tentative than before, reached him.

"You're going to catch the person who did this, right?"

"That's why we're here," he assured her. "The FBI brought us in all the way from Anchorage because Agents Nez and Lync, and their colleagues, have a lot of experience. This case is the only thing they're investigating right now. It's our biggest priority."

"That's not an answer," she said, more grief than anger in her words.

He nodded soberly. "I'm not going to make you a promise I can't guarantee. But I'll tell you this—we're putting everything we have into this investigation. And when it comes to finding bombers, the FBI is *very* good. I'd bet on us."

He stepped a little closer, wanting her to read on his face how much he believed it. "I can also promise to I'll keep you informed. I believe we'll get this person. You let us worry about that. You focus on getting better. Deal?"

She swiped a hand across her face, wiping away a rush of tears he pretended not to see. "Okay."

He gave her an encouraging smile, then followed Ben and Anderson into the hall.

It wasn't until they were outside the hospital that Ben halted suddenly, turning to face him and making Patches stop short. "You want to act like these victims' personal therapist, that's your business. I know you're good at your job, so I'm not going to question your methods. But Anderson and I know what we're doing, too. So let us do our jobs."

Jax put his hands up, pasted an innocent look on his face.

"We asked you to come along because it makes

the victims more comfortable. They connect with you and it reduces the stress of feeling like they need to give us information or we won't find the person who killed someone they love. Or the stress of having to relive what happened to them. We're happy to have you with us. But you're not an agent, Jax. You need to remember that."

Ben shook his head and spun around again, striding for the SUV.

Anderson gave Jax a sympathetic look, but he didn't disagree with his partner, just followed.

Patches stared up at him, reading the tension, and Jax stroked her soft fur. "You did a good job, Patches. I'm the one who's in trouble."

She shifted, pressing all sixty pounds against him. She wasn't that big, but she was strong.

He laughed, giving her an extra pat on the head. "Thanks, Patches. Let's get going."

She strode alongside him, her gait full of puppy energy. Sometimes, he forgot that at a year old, technically she still was a puppy. Despite the tough job he'd given her, despite the difficult start in life she'd had—being tossed onto the street to fend for herself at a few weeks old—she was always cheerful.

The perfect fit for a job like this. But sometimes the job still got to her.

Right now it was getting to him. And it wasn't talking to the victims, as hard as that was.

He'd come to the FBI from private therapy to

help stop perpetrators before they could become repeat offenders. He knew he made a difference here. But despite his training, despite how much he loved what he did, sometimes being a Victim Specialist felt too far on the sidelines.

Sometimes, it just didn't feel like he was doing enough.

THE STATION WAS empty and dark.

Normally, Keara would be gone by now. Actually, if things were normal, she probably wouldn't be working at all on a Sunday. But with worried citizens needing reassurance, and a town that needed extra vigilance because of a nearby bombing without an obvious motive, she'd come in early and stayed late.

Heading home didn't mean she was off the clock. In a small town like Desparre, there was no such thing as truly off the clock. If something happened after the station was officially closed for the night, the officer—or chief—who was closest to the action would get the first call.

Tonight she didn't want to get on the road. Didn't feel like making the relatively short drive to her house.

She'd been distracted all day, moving on autopilot. In a job like hers, that was dangerous. But knowing that didn't make it any easier to focus.

After she'd returned home from Luna last night, images of her life with Juan had taunted her sleep. She'd woken on a scream, on the memory of returning home from work that horrible day.

She'd been exhausted, frustrated by a case she hardly remembered, one she'd subsequently solved. She'd wanted nothing more than to settle on the couch in front of the TV with a delivery pizza and a bottle of red wine. To simply snuggle with her husband and forget the argument they'd been having on replay every few weeks.

The house had been lit up, the front door locked, no sign that anything was wrong. She'd walked inside and headed straight for the shower, a holdover habit from her days on patrol. Forensics said the timing wouldn't have mattered, that Juan had been dead before she even arrived home, but the shower still bothered her. The fact that she hadn't suspected for a second that anything was wrong, that she'd had no idea the man she'd loved so deeply was already gone.

And then, afterward, the hint of annoyance when she'd walked through the house and couldn't find him. The sigh she'd heaved as she'd realized the back door was open, that he hadn't bothered to come in from the garden when she'd arrived. The way she'd desperately tried to suck in gulps of air once she'd fallen to the ground beside him, but her lungs still screamed, telling her she wasn't getting enough oxygen.

The investigation had determined that someone

had hopped the fence into their backyard while Juan was relaxing on a lawn chair. They'd slipped up behind him and slit his throat.

If he'd realized anyone was there, the knowledge had come too late. There were no defense marks on his arms or hands. No awkward angle to the slice across his neck, which might have happened if he'd tried to turn at the last minute.

She hoped it meant that it had all happened too fast for him to suffer. But even an instant of pain, even a flash of insight that everything he'd fought for in his life was over, was too much.

It was too much for her, too. For six years being in Alaska had kept the memories at a survivable distance.

Now the bombing was bringing it all back. But if the person who'd killed Juan had come here and set off a bomb, why had he chosen such a different crime?

Fitz hadn't sent her the case file from Celia Harris's murder yet, but if that killer was responsible for the bomb, too, something drastic had changed. She'd seen the evidence photos from Celia's murder; the whole office had. They'd been gruesome enough, with such an unlikely victim, that Juan and Fitz had consulted briefly with the rest of the detectives.

Celia hadn't been killed in the alley where she'd been found, and her killer had taken his time murdering her. Although Keara's cases tended to be the standard sort—motivated by more obvious reasons like greed, jealousy or anger—Houston wasn't immune to serial killers. She'd understood immediately why Juan and Fitz had thought there'd be more murders.

But a bombing seven years later? Even if the bomber had stood nearby and watched the pain and death his handiwork caused, was it really the same as wielding a knife? She'd never heard of a violent killer becoming a bomber.

Maybe she was reaching, grasping at a similar symbol because she still needed answers, despite how far she'd run.

The crackle of the intercom from outside the entrance of the building, followed by a familiar voice asking "Keara? Er-Chief Hernandez?" startled her.

The distinctive voice made goose bumps prick her arms. Keara rubbed them away as she stood and strode to the front of the station, swinging the door wide.

"How did you know I was here?"

Woof! Patches answered, making a smile break through the mask of competence and calm that Keara used automatically on the job.

"Yours is the only civilian car in the lot."

He'd noticed what car she was driving? She studied him more closely, taking in the focused stare belied by a relaxed stance. Maybe psychologists were more like police officers than she'd thought, both needing to be observant and analytical.

"You have news on the bombing?" As she asked it, she realized the only reason he'd tell her in person was if it was connected to her past. Bracing her hand on the open door frame, she asked, "Is it connected to my husband's death?"

"What?" Jax's too-serious expression morphed into concern as he took a step closer.

Too late, she remembered that he knew her husband had investigated a murder where the symbol was found, but not much more. He didn't know anything about Rodney Brown, or the fact that her husband's murder had never been solved. Or even the fact that her husband's death had been a murder.

She took a step back, losing the stability of holding on to the door frame, but also escaping Jax's cinnamony scent. She didn't know if it was aftershave or cologne or if he just liked to mainline chai, but it was the sort of scent she wanted to keep breathing in.

It was distracting. *He* was distracting.

Something bumped her leg and Keara looked down, finding Patches there. The dog had followed her inside. Jax was coming, too, but moving more slowly.

Keara kept her gaze on Patches, petting the dog while she tried to come up with a way to redirect Jax, a way to avoid talking about what had happened to Juan.

"I don't have anything new to share about the bombing," Jax said, his voice slow and soft. "And Anderson is still waiting on that file from Houston PD. Is there more you need to tell me? Some other connection we should investigate?"

When she didn't immediately answer, he put his hand under her elbow.

The contact startled her, warmth from his hand making her realize how cold the rest of her body felt. She jerked her gaze back up to his. "Maybe. I'll know more once I get a look at that case file."

Jax stared at her, his dark brown eyes hypnotic. Finally, he nodded, stepping just slightly closer.

She had to tilt her head back to hold eye contact and she put a warning in her gaze. She liked Jax, but she'd been a police officer too long not to see what was coming. He was trying to make a connection, sympathize with her so she'd trust him enough to tell him what he needed to know.

A slight smile tilted his lips and Keara wondered if she needed to put a different kind of "back off" vibe out there. Nerves fluttered in her chest and she put it down to how long it had been since she'd had to let anyone down easy. Since she was their police chief, thankfully, people here mostly considered her off-limits as a woman.

"I'm not an agent."

His words were so far from what she'd expected to hear that it took her a few extra seconds to digest them.

"And you have no jurisdiction in Luna," he continued.

She crossed her arms over her chest, refusing to take a step backward and let him know his closeness affected her. "And?"

"The case you talked about feels psychologically different—the MO, the location, everything. But I can't get that symbol out of my head. It might have been an accident that we were able to recover it on the bomb, but it wasn't an accident that the bomber made it. It means something to him. That suggests the cases are connected somehow. I can't let this go. And since you're waiting on a case file you really shouldn't be requesting, I'm guessing you can't, either."

Keara frowned, trying to keep her expression neutral as Patches nudged her leg, looking for attention. Despite all the memories that had resurfaced tonight, she couldn't help but smile at the dog, with her tiny matching brown spots at the top of each eyebrow, and bigger spots on her muzzle and chest. Keara silently pet Patches again as she waited for Jax to continue.

"I think we should work together," Jax finished, staring at her expectantly. "Quietly, on the side. If we come up with anything, we share it with the agents."

It was a mistake for a lot of reasons.

Keeping information from the investigating agents—no matter how small or seemingly inconsequential—could be the difference that prevented the case from being solved. Besides, if she and Jax worked outside the official team, they wouldn't have all of the information.

After this was over, Jax would go back to Anchorage, but she still had to live in this community. She'd have to answer to her citizens if something went wrong, and she'd lose the support of their closest neighboring town, too.

Then there was Jax himself. Although she had no concerns when it came to her self-control around the handsome Victim Specialist, she couldn't deny that he ignited a tiny flicker of attraction whenever he was near.

Juan had been gone for seven years. She wasn't totally closed off to the idea of moving on someday. But it didn't feel like the time, not even for a fling. Not if this case could be the key to solving his murder.

"Okay," she agreed, the word bursting free before she could hold it back. "Let's work together."

Chapter Six

Something was wrong.

Jax could see it through the window of the tiny diner on the outskirts of Desparre, somewhere Keara had told him they were less likely to attract attention. It had been an hour drive for him after spending the day all over Luna with Ben and Anderson, talking to victims and families. He'd left discouraged and exhausted, with the bruises on his back and legs aching, but judging from the unguarded torment on her face, Keara's day had been worse.

He pictured the look on her face yesterday when she'd asked if the bombing was connected to her husband's death. That meant her husband had been murdered—and presumably, that the murder had never been solved. He'd desperately wanted to ask about it, but he couldn't turn off years of working as a psychologist. It had been the wrong time. But maybe today would be different.

"Come on, Patches," he said, leading the way into the diner. Keara had told him that the owner was low-key and didn't mind letting working dogs inside.

True to her promise, the diner was mostly empty and the waitress who nodded a greeting just cooed "aww" when she spotted Patches.

By the time Jax joined Keara at her booth, she looked serious and in control. The ability to mask her emotions that fast was probably a necessary skill for a police chief. But it still surprised him. And if he was being honest with himself, he was a little disappointed that she felt the need to hide from him.

You barely know her, he reminded himself. Yes, people usually opened up to him faster, probably because knowing how to reach people was a job requirement he couldn't just turn off outside work. And yes, last night they'd agreed to work together, so he'd expected more honesty. But mostly, he was just intrigued by her. He had no idea how long he'd have to get to know her before the case was solved and he had to go back to Anchorage.

"Is anything wrong?" Jax asked, keeping his voice neutral.

Patches took the more direct route. She went to Keara's side of the booth and put her head on the seat.

From the surprise and amusement on Keara's face, Patches had looked up at Keara with her soft puppy eyes, a tactic that rarely failed.

The smile twitching at the corners of Keara's lips burst into a true grin as she pet Patches. "She really knows how to put on the charm, doesn't she? Is that something you taught her when you trained her to work for the FBI?"

"Nah, she came by that naturally. I was biking home from work one day and—"

"You *biked* to work in Anchorage? Must have been summer."

"This was almost a year ago. I was working in DC then. Getting to and from FBI headquarters took forever in traffic, so I bought a bike. Anyway, I was on my way home and I saw something moving in the bushes and then this tiny little puppy jumped out. She gave me this look like she wanted me to take her home."

He'd had to swerve his bike, had almost tipped it. But he'd always felt like she'd been waiting for him to come along.

Growing up, he'd had a dog, so he'd known instantly that Patches was too young to be away from her mother. But she'd been totally alone, so he'd scooped her up, walked his bike the rest of the way home and then taken her to a vet.

Keara's smile curled downward. "Someone left her out there?"

"Yeah."

She shook her head, still petting Patches. "Kids and animals," she muttered. "Those are the worst calls, because they're trusting, relying on someone to care for them. Not that I want to get called to any scene where someone is hurt, but at least as an adult, you've seen enough of the world to know. If you're paying attention, there are threats everywhere."

She was staring at his dog when she spoke, letting Jax study her more closely. He'd worked with law enforcement long enough to know how terrible their jobs could be. He wondered how being a chief in Desparre compared to being a detective in Houston. The latter was surely bloodier, but the former put a lot of responsibility on her shoulders.

Deciding to keep the conversation light, he continued, "It's lucky I found Patches when I did. The vet thought she was about six weeks old. But she was feisty and determined from the start. I'd been working for the FBI for two and a half years by then and there are a few Victim Specialists who have therapy dogs in DC. I immediately thought she'd be good at it. She officially started at six months. Youngest dog they've ever used."

He heard the pride in his voice as Keara's gaze finally swung back to him. There was something pensive in her gaze, something that made him want to lean across the table and get a little closer.

"Can I get you anything?"

The nasally voice startled Jax and he realized the waitress was standing next to their table.

"Just a coffee would be great."

"Make it two, please," Keara said.

"And for her?" The waitress nodded at his dog, then smiled. "Does she want a bowl of water? Or we can bring her a dog c-o-o-k-i-e."

Woof! Patches's head appeared over the top of the table, swiveled toward the waitress.

The waitress laughed. "I see she spells. Okay, two coffees and a dog cookie it is!"

When she left, Jax returned his attention to Keara. But whatever he'd seen in her eyes was gone now, replaced by a seriousness that told him they were about to get to work.

"So the woman who was murdered seven years ago? Celia Harris? Apparently, Juan, my husband, and his partner, Fitz, had a possible suspect. I mean, they looked at a lot of people and I guess this guy didn't stand out more than anyone else, at least not initially. But then, a week after my husband was murdered, Fitz went to talk to him again. I think it was kind of a distraction assignment, honestly, to reinterview any witnesses or suspects that Juan had talked to alone. You see, Fitz wanted to be part of the investigation into Juan's death and the chief wouldn't let him."

She didn't have to tell him that she'd also tried to insert herself into the investigation of her husband's murder. Just talking about it was making her eyes narrow and her lips tighten.

"What happened to your husband, Keara?"

"He was murdered." Her expression became even more pinched. "In our own backyard."

"I'm sorry."

"Me, too." She straightened, and he saw her game face come on. "It was never solved, which is why…" She took a visible breath, shook her head and started over, her voice calmer. "So about a week before he was killed, Juan went to talk to Rodney Brown. His car was pictured close to the scene near the time of Celia's murder. Fitz said Juan returned from that interview without feeling like he'd gained much, but the guy lied about the car being near the scene. And when Fitz went back—a week after my husband's throat was slit—the place was totally cleared out."

Jax felt himself cringe at Keara's description of how her husband had died. He could tell from the anger and pain wrapped up in those few words that she'd been the one to find him. An ache formed in his chest as he watched her, trying to be clinical. How much worse must it have been, as an officer of the law, knowing the person who'd killed him had gotten away with it?

"Fitz spent a lot of time trying to track down Rodney Brown. Apparently, he worked as an orderly at a hospital in Houston, but he just stopped showing up. His work history before that was a little spotty, so it wasn't totally out of character. And his family told Fitz that he was flighty and not great about staying in touch. Back then none of them were all that surprised that he'd just cleared out of his apartment. Fitz has been checking for signs of him over the years, even got a warrant to watch his credit report to see if he popped up somewhere else in the country. But there's been nothing."

"So you think he killed Celia Harris and your husband, too?"

"It's pretty suspicious timing to disappear."

"Yeah, it is."

"And now there's a bomb here with the same symbol. But…" She frowned, shook her head.

"You're thinking the same thing the FBI is," Jax concluded.

Her eyes narrowed at him, but she held off on saying anything as the waitress dropped off their coffees, and Patches started greedily chewing on her dog biscuit.

After the woman was gone, Keara demanded, "What do they think?"

"They don't know about your husband. No one from Houston mentioned that angle. And I'm guessing Rodney Brown's name is in the file, but he didn't stand out. The main thing is that—"

"A violent killer—someone who obviously enjoys the kill itself—is unlikely to become a bomber?"

"Pretty much," Jax confirmed. "You're right that the symbols are eerily similar. But if it's the same person, why a bomb? And why here? Why *now*, so many years after the murder in Texas?"

FITZ WAS RIGHT. Rodney Brown was a ghost.

Keara leaned back on her couch and took a sip

of red wine. It had been another long day, full of questions from her citizens that she couldn't answer, full of worry about a case she wasn't even supposed to be investigating. She wasn't usually much of a drinker, especially while she was pondering a case, but tonight she was on her second glass.

Maybe that was why she reached for her wedding album, instead of returning to her laptop. In those first months after Juan's death, she'd sobbed over the pages. But since moving to Alaska, she'd tucked it into the corner of her bookshelf and hadn't opened it again.

Now she ran her finger over the shape of Juan's face, frozen in a slightly nervous smile as he waited at the altar for her. When she'd first met him in that Houston roll call, seen the way his shoulders slumped and his mouth tightened at hearing he'd be partnered with her, she'd been sure they'd never be friends. But after a year of tough calls, patrolling a dangerous area together, they'd developed a mutual respect that had slowly blossomed into more.

Now he was gone. The constant, overwhelming grief she'd felt in that first year after he died had slowly dulled into something she could push to the back of her mind. But with each day that passed since she'd seen that blasted symbol, the gnawing ache was returning, along with the certainty that she'd failed Juan.

Fitz was right. She'd played by the rules in Houston, let her fellow detectives handle the case because she'd been sure they'd find justice for one of their own. And because it had been hard enough to function at all during those early days and months, let alone constantly look at pictures and details of what had happened to Juan. When the case had gone cold, she should have taken it up herself and damn the rules, damn the consequences. Instead, she'd run away.

Since coming to Alaska, she'd followed the rules, too. She'd tried to be a by-the-book chief. But not anymore.

She took another long sip of wine and closed the album, pushed it away from her. Tipping back the rest of her glass, she yanked the laptop into her lap and stared at the notes she'd compiled on Rodney Brown.

The guy was a loser. He'd had a handful of arrests as a minor for getting into fights. More of the same as an adult, usually bar fights. Plus a single sexual assault charge that had later been dropped. From what Keara could tell, it was more because the victim didn't want to go through a trial than for lack of evidence.

Serial killers were often sexually motivated. But Celia Harris hadn't been sexually assaulted. Fitz's investigation had never turned up any similar kills. Although Rodney Brown clearly had a violent streak and a problem with women, there were no signs he'd ever crossed paths with Celia Harris. And he didn't seem sophisticated enough to have pulled off the risky abduction and then committed such a violent murder without leaving behind useful evidence.

Juan's murder had been almost professional. A quick hit and then the killer had disappeared. No one in her neighborhood had noticed anyone who didn't belong or seen anyone running away at the time of the murder. Yes, it made sense that a violent killer of women who thought the police were onto him might try and take out the detective who'd questioned him.

But Rodney Brown had only been questioned once. After a few weeks of silence, would he seek Juan out and murder him? The closer she looked at the details of the case, the more unlikely that idea seemed. Taking all of the pieces together, she understood why Fitz had decided the two weren't connected.

Except the timing was pretty hard to ignore. And the fact that Rodney Brown had so completely dropped off the map suggested a sophistication that perhaps he'd hidden in the rest of his life.

As for the bomb, sure, anyone could dig up the basics on the internet. But pulling it off was another thing. And no matter how she looked at it, the long gap in time and the change in MO made it pretty unlikely that all three crimes were connected.

Cursing, she tossed her laptop onto the couch beside her. Tears of frustration blurred her vision, but she blinked them back.

Yes, cold cases were harder than fresh investigations. The adage of the "first forty-eight hours" was true. Over time, memories faded, witnesses forgot, evidence that had been missed the first time often disappeared for good. But that didn't make them impossible.

Keara pictured the symbol from Anderson's phone, with the series of interconnecting loops, drawn onto the bomb with a thick black marker. Different enough from the symbol over Celia's body in that alley, spray-painted onto the stucco wall of the adjacent building in bloodred. But the design itself was the same, the loops that looked almost childish. If all of this was connected, if she had a shot at solving her husband's murder, that symbol was the key.

The melodic ring of her doorbell startled her, made her glance at the credenza in the corner where she'd stashed her weapon. Few people knew exactly where she lived. Even fewer would visit.

She considered ignoring it, but curiosity got the better of her and she strode to the door. When she peered through the peephole, there was Jax on her front porch, shivering in a dark coat and looking tired. Patches was at his side, her head swiveling from him to the door, as if she knew Keara had stepped up to the other side.

It had been a long time since she'd felt attracted to someone. Sure, she'd had brief flashes of awareness in Alaska when she crossed paths with someone, but nothing that lasted more than a few minutes. With Jax, the attraction seemed to grow each time she saw him, with each new detail she noticed. The surprising muscles in his arms when he'd stripped down to a T-shirt in the hotel lobby, the intuitiveness of his gaze when she was holding something back, the hint of a dimple that popped on his right cheek when he gave a full-blown grin, usually at Patches.

More than simple attraction, though, she felt a *connection* with Jax. Some invisible pull, a desire to simply sit beside him and soak in his presence. She'd tried to ignore the feeling, but right now she felt that pull even more than usual.

"It's the wine," she muttered, resting her forehead against the door, anxious at such a simple decision. Open the door and let him in? Or pretend not to be home?

Woof!

A smile burst free and Keara had to smother the giggle that wanted to follow. Any man who could inspire such loyalty from a dog like Patches had to be a good one. And maybe the fact that he lived so far away was a plus. Anchorage was definitely past the point of being practical for a relationship, so that alone should avoid any awkwardness when it was time for him to leave.

He might be FBI, but he wasn't a law-enforcement officer. He wasn't in the thick of danger, wasn't someone she'd have to constantly worry about.

Not that it really mattered. She didn't want anything serious. Not now. Probably never again.

But a fling with a handsome, intelligent, sensitive man? Maybe it was time.

Taking a deep breath, Keara opened the door.

Chapter Seven

The door swung open and Keara swayed forward, her gaze locked on his and lips parted. He'd never seen her hair down before, but right now it hung long, silky and loose, perfectly straight over her shoulders. She was dressed casually, in jeans and a well-worn long-sleeved T-shirt that looked soft to the touch and showed off curves her police uniform hid. Even her expression was less guarded, softer.

"Come in," she said, her voice huskier than usual.

Patches bounded inside at the invitation, but warning bells went off in Jax's head, despite the desire stirring in his belly.

He could see it in her low-lidded gaze. She thought he was here for a totally different reason than the agreed-upon plan to investigate together. Of course, she'd never given him her address, never invited him over. It had been foolish to show up without calling. Especially at nine o' clock at night.

But after yet another day of nonstop visits with victims and family members, feeling no closer to bringing any of them real closure, he'd just wanted to see Keara. To sit across from her and watch the way her lips pursed when she was deep in thought, see the determination in her gaze and posture when she thought she was onto something. To soak up her presence and soothe his own frustrated nerves.

So he'd managed to get her home address out of Luna's police chief, under the pretense that he was keeping her apprised of the investigation, and she was keeping them informed of anything suspicious in Desparre.

It had been stupid and selfish, he realized now as Keara raised her eyebrows at him, the corners of her lips twisting up in an expression that looked like a dare. Red wine stained her lips with a hint of purple.

He tried to come up with an excuse to leave, but then she licked those lips and he was moving forward without conscious intent.

She pushed the door closed behind him, leaning against him as she did it, and the brief contact made his mouth go dry.

This close, he could see the ring of slightly lighter brown at the center of her coffee-colored irises. He could smell a rich cabernet, subtle enough that he doubted she'd drank a lot. And it wasn't just her well-worn T-shirt that was soft; it was also her skin.

She blinked up at him, her chest rising and falling faster, and he could feel his own breathing pick up in response.

He'd been drawn to her from the first day

they'd met. So when she swayed forward again—or had he leaned toward her?—he ignored the voice in his head telling him this was the wrong time. Threading his fingers through hers, he tugged gently and then she was pressing against him, up on her tiptoes.

The first contact of her lips sent a spark through his body like he'd given himself an electric shock. Then he closed his mouth around her bottom lip and tasted the cabernet she'd been drinking.

She let out a noise that was half-sigh, half-moan and pushed higher on her toes, her free hand tangling in his hair and pulling him closer. Then her tongue was in his mouth and her kisses turned fast and frantic.

Jax wrapped his free hand around her back, molding her body to his, and his heart rate skyrocketed. He had a solid seven inches on her and yet somehow, the fit was perfect.

Woof!

Patches's bark registered in the back of his mind as Keara kissed him harder.

Then Patches let out several more, higher pitched barks.

The insistent sound returned him to reality, helped his mind take the lead back over from his body. He pulled away slightly, trying to catch his breath as he stared over Keara's head and down the hall.

Patches stood in Keara's hallway, leaning

slightly forward, as if ready to bark again or run toward them.

Unwinding his arm from around Keara's back, Jax tried to calm his pounding heart. The scent of her—a mix of that wine with something sweeter and more subtle—invaded his senses, making it hard to focus, especially when she leaned in again.

He stepped back, quickly enough that she stumbled toward him before righting herself.

"This probably isn't a good idea," he forced himself to say.

Keara blinked at him a few times, then that professional mask slipped back over her features. But not before he saw a flash of hurt in her eyes.

She was as attracted to him as he was to her. But he'd be a terrible psychologist if he didn't recognize that they were both acting on it for the wrong reasons.

Flings weren't his thing. They never had been, but at thirty-eight years old, he felt way past them. And even if Keara was emotionally available, she lived four hundred miles away. He might be here for a month or a break might come in the case tomorrow and that fast, he'd be on a flight home.

Besides, Keara hadn't kissed him because of that attraction. She'd kissed him because she was emotional and frustrated, probably over the thread-thin connection between her husband's death and the bombing.

He took another step away from her, as the idea of her kissing him because she missed her dead husband cooled the rest of his desire.

"You came to talk about the case?" Keara asked, her voice as detached and remote as the expression on her face.

When he nodded, she spun and headed into the interior of her house. "Come on, then."

As soon as she reached Patches, the dog turned to walk with her. Keara stroked Patches's head as they strode away, his dog's tail wagging.

Running a hand through his hair, straightening the spots where Keara had tugged and tangled it, he followed. With every step, he took a deep breath, trying not to watch the sway of her hips as she led him into her living room.

It was exactly what he would have expected her personal space to be. Cozy, with a fireplace centered in the room. Comfortable, with a couch that looked perfect for curling up on. There was even a wool blanket thrown over the back of it. And peaceful, with big curtained windows diagonal from the fireplace that had to open to a spectacular view of the forest behind her.

There was an open bottle of wine and a single empty wineglass on the live-edge wood coffee table. Beside it, a laptop and a wedding album.

A mix of regret and pain—some for her, some for himself—tensed his chest and then dropped to his stomach.

Her gaze went from him to the album, then back again. "If there's a connection between all of this, it's that symbol. We need to know what it means." Her expression gave nothing away, but her voice was slightly shaky as she sank onto the couch. "You've got a psychology background, right? Any ideas?"

Jax settled on the big leather chair beside the couch, not surprised when Patches pushed past him to sit beside Keara. His dog always knew who needed her most.

"That's profiler territory," Jax said. "I used to be a psychologist, so yeah, I definitely have insight into some of these criminals. But this symbol doesn't represent anything I can decode."

"It's the only thing connecting the crimes," Keara said, the frustration in her voice edged with grief. "Nothing else is similar. Fitz sent me the file from Celia Harris's murder. And I know everything about Juan's murder. The only possible link is the timing and the fact that Juan questioned a possible witness shortly before he was killed—and shortly before that witness disappeared. But the bombing? Nothing about it seems remotely connected. Except this damn symbol."

Jax leaned forward in his chair, resting his forearms on his thighs. "What if that's because the murder—or possibly murders, if your husband's case is also connected—were the anomaly? What if he was always a bomber?"

Keara twisted slightly to face him, her eyebrows twitching inward. At her interest, Patches pivoted, too. "What do you mean?"

"Maybe the kill was personal. Maybe the bomber knew Celia Harris. Maybe bombs are his thing and this was the exception." He could hear the excitement in his voice as he turned it over in his mind. "It could make him easier to track if he's really a bomber. Maybe there have been others."

Keara's shoulders dropped, her excitement obviously waning. "I don't think so. Juan thought Rodney was suspicious mainly because he so vehemently denied being near the crime scene when it happened. But he couldn't find any personal connection between Rodney and Celia. If this was a serial killer, that wouldn't matter so much. But a personal kill?" She shook her head. "After Juan died and Rodney disappeared, Fitz dug deep, looking for a connection. He never found one, either."

"You said Rodney was flighty, right? That he didn't tend to stay in one place for long, that even his family wasn't all that concerned when he cleared out?"

"Sure, but it's pretty coincidental timing," Keara insisted.

"Exactly," Jax agreed. "What if Rodney leaving *is* just a coincidence? Maybe Celia's murder and this bombing are connected. And it's possible your husband's death is, too. *Maybe*. But what if it's not Rodney? What if we're looking for someone else?"

"WHAT IF IT'S not Rodney?"

Jax's words from last night had run through Keara's mind during a restless night of sleep and again duringher drive into work this morning—when she wasn't distracted by memories of kissing him. She'd been attracted to him from the start, so she'd expected to enjoy those kisses. What she hadn't expected was the intensity.

The man kissed with a singular focus, until she'd felt consumed by the feel of him, by the taste of him. He might not have been law enforcement, but after plastering herself against him, she suspected he worked out with his agent colleagues, because his chest was rock-solid.

It was better that he'd stopped it before things went too far.

He was a colleague. He was also her best chance at connecting the Luna bombing to her husband's murder—if in fact they were connected.

He was also dangerous. A fling was one thing. A fling was temporary, a distraction from the fact that she'd chosen a profession that sucked away a lot of her personal time. A distraction from the fact that even if she had more personal time, she had no one to spend it with. But a single kiss from Jax and she'd felt herself wanting. Physical wanting, of course. But emotional wanting, too. And that was territory she didn't want to revisit.

"Everything okay, Chief?"

Keara looked up from her desk.

Tate Emory was standing in her doorway, too-perceptive concern in his dark eyes. He was the closest thing she had to a friend on the force. Not that she didn't like just about everyone on her team, but Tate was different. She knew his secret, had given him a job in a tricky situation, so it was easier to share things with him in return. She'd kept his confidence, so he'd keep hers.

But not this. Not the guilt that filled her like nausea when she thought about kissing Jax when she should have been focused on getting justice for Juan.

She forced a smile. "It's been a tough week. We're four days out from that bomb and neither the FBI nor the Luna police have much more to go on than they did when it went off."

By Wednesday morning— a full ninety-six hours after the bomb had detonated—she'd expected a solid suspect, maybe even an arrest, but at the very least, a manhunt. Instead, the FBI's semiregular news conferences beside Luna's police chief focused more on reassuring a scared public that they were working on it, and asking them to come forward if they had information that could help.

What the public didn't know—what Keara had learned from talking to her colleagues in the Luna Police Department—was that the FBI still had a long way to go. They still had no idea who or what the intended target was, or what goal the bomber was trying to accomplish. Was there a message? If so, no one knew what it was. They still weren't even sure if the bomber had been going for a bigger death toll by waiting until the impromptu soccer game happened or if that was unintentional and he'd expected few—or maybe even no—dead.

"Hey, at least it's finally May," Tate said, his tone more enthusiastic than the forty-five-degree weather warranted.

It would be a while before they hit temperatures that didn't require a coat. But at least it was sunny.

She gave him a halfhearted smile, acknowledging his attempt to cheer her up.

"I'm going to take a trek up the mountain today," Tate said, apparently giving up on that.

"Take Lorenzo and Nate with you. I doubt we're going to magically run across someone who knows something, but let's be honest. If Desparre is a good place to hide out, the mountain takes it to the next level."

The mountain that separated Desparre from Luna was a great place to get lost, even more lost than the relative isolation offered by the rest of

Desparre. Five years ago they'd discovered kidnappers had hidden five kids on that mountain for many years. They'd also found a murderer, running from a decades-old charge in Kansas. It wasn't a stretch to imagine a bomber hiding there, too.

All of her officers were using their extra time between calls to chat with citizens, both to reassure them that the bombing investigation would be solved and also to see if anyone had useful information. So far it hadn't borne any fruit, but there had to be a reason the bomber had targeted such a tiny park. Luna and Desparre weren't that far apart, at least not in Alaskan terms. So there was a good chance someone around here knew something, even if they didn't realize it.

Lorenzo Riera was one of her veterans, a steady officer who'd once faced down a grizzly bear who'd gotten a taste for people food and wandered downtown four years ago. He'd just as readily had her back at a more standard bar fight breakup last month. His partner, Nate Dreymond, had barely passed a year on the force. Since Tate's partner, Peter, had left a few months ago, Nate was the force's rookie.

Having Lorenzo at his side would be good backup for Tate if he ran into trouble, and having Nate tag along would give the rookie a chance to watch two great officers at work.

"Got it," Tate agreed. "But you know, maybe

you should reconsider the K-9 unit. If I had a K-9 partner, you wouldn't have to keep putting out those failed job postings for another officer."

It was a request Tate had been making almost from his first day on the force. Usually, Keara cited their lack of funds. But after seeing Jax work with Patches, she wondered if the cost might be worth it. "I'll think about it."

Tate's mouth opened and closed, as if her response had totally thrown him.

"Let me know if anything pops," she said.

He nodded and took the cue to leave.

She should do the same. Being chief meant a certain amount of politics and paperwork, but in a town as small as Desparre, it still required her to be out on the streets, too. Or maybe that was just the kind of chief she'd chosen to be.

She'd been out in her town every day since the bomb had gone off, reassuring citizens and doing the same kind of low-key investigative work as her officers. But right now the question of Rodney Brown's involvement was still messing with her focus.

Jax's claim that Rodney's leaving was just coincidence could be right. Twelve years in law enforcement had taught her that stranger coincidences happened. The problem was, it had also taught her to always be suspicious of them, because too much of a coincidence usually meant it wasn't actually a coincidence.

Then again, maybe something bad had happened to Rodney, too. But what? And why?

Rodney Brown killing Celia Harris and then killing Juan was a real possibility she couldn't drop. But the bombing connection felt more tenuous.

What if they were two different people? The idea made Keara jerk straighter in her chair, making it roll slightly backward and bump the credenza behind her.

Two different people didn't mean they weren't connected.

The theory made her heart rate pick up, sent a familiar rush through her body. The thrill of the chase, when her gut was screaming she'd hit on something. She'd felt it regularly as a detective. As a chief, she had less opportunity to be in the center of a case in the same way.

Grabbing her cell phone, she hit redial on a number that had started to appear constantly on her list of recent calls.

"Jax Diallo."

The deep, relaxing tone of his voice sent a little thrill through her that Keara tried to ignore. "Jax, it's Keara."

"Keara."

The way he said her name, the way she could practically see his slight smile, made her stomach clench. Pushing forward, she told him her new theory. "What if you're right about Celia Harris's murder being personal? What if the person who killed her is still out there, but it's not Rodney Brown?"

"I don't—"

She kept talking, adrenaline pumping, her words spilling out faster as the idea continued to take shape. "What if the killer knew Rodney, knew the symbol he liked to use, and spray-painted it above Celia's body to lead police in the wrong direction? Or maybe they'd had a falling out and it was a 'screw you' kind of move?"

"So you're suggesting Rodney is the bomber?" Jax asked, not sounding anywhere near as excited by the theory as she felt.

"Yes! When Juan came to talk to him about the murder, he was pissed because his symbol was used. He killed Juan to keep him from connecting it to his own crimes. Then he left town."

"So you think Juan is the one who let it slip about the symbol? But what about Rodney's car being near the murder scene?" Jax asked, still sounding confused.

"We know Rodney was near there at the time of the killing. Maybe it really was coincidence. Or maybe he knew what was going to happen and drove by, but he wasn't the killer."

"Then, the real killer told Rodney he was going to murder this woman? Why would he do that?"

"Maybe they had a sick friendship. You can't tell me you haven't seen criminals connect before, give each other ideas, trade stories about what they've done, even cooperate with each other. Maybe give each other alibis. Maybe play a one-upmanship game."

"Well, sure," Jax said, his tone still skeptical.

"Maybe that's what happened here," Keara said, holding in her frustration. "And whether or not Juan mentioned the symbol, Rodney knew about it. So maybe that was his real worry. He wouldn't know that Houston PD isn't like the FBI. We don't have bomb databases. We wouldn't know if he'd used that symbol before, not if it was outside our jurisdiction."

She blew out a heavy breath, tried to slow her adrenaline along with the speed of her words. "What I'm saying, Jax, is that maybe the killer and the bomber *aren't* the same person. But maybe they know each other, even schemed together at one point. And Rodney killed my husband because he was onto something bigger than a single murder."

Jax sighed. "It's a good theory, Keara, but there's a problem."

"What?"

"The FBI ran the bombing details through our database, specifically that symbol. They finished reviewing everything today and confirmed it. We've never seen a bomb with this symbol before. Not in Houston, not anywhere."

Chapter Eight

With every large-scale crime scene, Jax found at least one person whose resilience awed him. From the Luna bombing, that person was Gabi Sinclair.

The young woman was a fighter. She'd lost a leg, lost a fiancé. She was definitely angry, grieving and in pain, but she was also strong. She had a lot still to get through, but he knew she'd come out the other side of it.

He went to see Gabi at her mom's house in Desparre, where she was staying while she healed. He was hoping she might remember something more, since she'd been at the edge of the park, maybe at a good vantage point to see the bomber leave the scene. But she had nothing new to offer him, just like he had nothing new to share about the investigation. The most he was able to do was return her fiancé's watch, which had been processed by the FBI.

"They told me in a month, I'll get a preparatory prosthetic," Gabi said, fighting through the pain as she settled herself on her mom's couch, with Patches beside her good leg. "After a few months I'll be able to get fitted for something permanent. Then I'm going to learn to run again."

She said it all with her chin tipped high, with her mom clutching her hand and fighting tears.

Gabi only broke down once, when he handed her the watch and she told him about her fiancé's funeral, which had been put on hold long enough for Gabi to be released from the hospital.

As Jax and Patches climbed into his rental SUV, Gabi's broken words echoed in his head. "I thought Carter and I had so much time. We had so many plans. Now all our dreams for our future together are just gone."

Instead of seeing Gabi's tearful gaze, he pictured Keara, stoic and frustrated as she tried to get closure, seven long years after her husband had been murdered.

It wasn't his job. Not to investigate the bombing outside his role with the victims. Definitely not to try and connect it to an old murder case. But he'd seen what a good investigation could do for those left behind. Knowing who was to blame, being able to see justice done for those they loved. It made a difference. It was why he'd left private practice to join the FBI. Maybe he could help Keara find her own closure.

"Call Keara Hernandez," he told his phone as he started up his SUV, heading toward downtown Desparre instead of back to Luna. Even before she picked up, his pulse increased at the thought of seeing her.

"Hello?"

Her tone was cautious, as if she wasn't sure what to expect, and he wondered if it was because of their kiss last night or his less-than-enthusiastic response to her theory this morning.

"I'm in Desparre and I was hoping we could grab a coffee before I make the drive back to Luna," he told her, surprised at the nerves in his belly, like he was asking for a date instead of a chance to talk about the case.

He could have just swung by the police station, but he didn't want word getting around that he was spending too much time talking to the Desparre police chief. Ben and Anderson were already suspicious. As much as he respected them, he wasn't in the mood for their only-partially joking jabs at him "playing agent." Especially since he didn't plan to stop. Not for this case, and not when it might help Keara.

When the pause on the other end of the phone went on too long, Patches chimed in. *Woof! Woof!*

Keara laughed. "Okay, Patches. I can do that." Then her voice got more businesslike. "This isn't Anchorage. We don't have a dedicated coffee shop in Desparre. But there's a spot we can go outside downtown with good coffee. You have a new idea about the case?"

"I wish I did. I just thought we could talk it over again, see if we can come up with something new." He didn't say the rest of it: he wanted to see her.

There was another pause, like Keara was reconsidering, but then she said, "Okay," and gave him an address.

It was actually closer to Gabi's mom's place than driving all the way into downtown, and Jax pulled into a gas station and did a quick U-turn to get onto a different street. According to his GPS, it was a quicker route to The Lodge, the spot where Keara had recommended they meet.

"You ready to see Keara?" he asked Patches, glancing at her in his rearview mirror.

As she barked an affirmative, Jax frowned, squinting at the huge dark blue truck behind him. It looked like the same vehicle that had been behind him on the road from Gabi's. But why would it now be going this way? Had it also turned around at the gas station?

Was someone following him? And why did that vehicle seem slightly familiar, like he'd seen it before today?

He eased up on the gas, slowing to ten miles below the limit, hoping the truck would pass him on the otherwise deserted road. But it slowed, too, staying just far enough behind him that Jax couldn't get a good look at the driver.

His heart rate picked up, even as he told himself he was being paranoid. Why would anyone follow him?

It was probably just a coincidence. Still, when a street appeared to his right, Jax yanked the wheel that way.

Patches barked and he could hear her sliding across the seat at his sudden turn.

"Sorry, Patches," Jax said, his gaze darting back and forth between the road ahead and the rearview mirror.

After a minute passed and the truck didn't appear again, Jax let out a heavy breath and eased his foot slightly off the gas.

Despite telling himself he'd been overreacting, he didn't fully relax until he reached the restaurant Keara had chosen. Apparently, it had once been a lodge and even the outside looked more like a log cabin than a small-town restaurant.

As he let Patches out of the SUV and scratched her ears, an apology for his erratic driving, he couldn't help glancing around for the big blue truck. Then he shook his head and muttered, "I think I needed a longer break, Patches."

She stared up at him, her soft brown eyes telegraphing sympathy.

He'd considered taking a vacation between finishing his term on the Rapid Deployment Team in DC and moving out to Anchorage. But the job opening had seemed perfect and the idea of Alaska had felt so different and enticing that he'd jumped on it. He'd been sure the cases he'd see here would be tiny compared to the mass casualty events that had burned him out over the previous three years. But this bombing was bringing it all back.

Apparently, that stress was making him imagine threats where there were none.

Movement in the distance made him jump and his gaze darted to the woods bracketing the restaurant. Then he froze in awe.

A moose, much bigger than he'd imagined the animals to be, paused and stared back at him.

When Patches took a slow, curious step forward, Jax grabbed her collar and his rapid movement sent the moose running.

Letting go of a breath along with Patches's collar, he said, "Let's go see Keara."

Woof! Woof!

Grinning at his dog's suddenly wagging tail, echoing his own feelings, Jax led her into The Lodge. There were small tables scattered throughout the main space, centered around a fireplace. Near the front was a section that carried food, like a small specialty grocery store.

It wasn't very big, so he could tell immediately that despite his detour, he'd still beaten Keara here. Probably due to his erratic driving. Good thing there hadn't been a cop around to pull him over for speeding. That would have been embarrassing—and not just because Keara would have heard about it.

Jax ordered himself a chai latte, while the teenage girl behind the counter cooed at Patches, and then he sat at one of the cozy tables. It looked like a spot to take a date, not the sort of place you'd sit and talk about an old murder and a new bombing.

His nerves picked up again, for an entirely different reason, as Keara entered the restaurant. She spotted him across the room, a hesitant smile tipping her lips before she turned and ordered herself a drink.

Then she was walking toward him and Jax couldn't stop himself from cataloging all the differences from last night. Her hair was tied up in its typical tight bun and as she unzipped her coat, he discovered she was wearing her police uniform. Everything about her—including the serious look on her face—broadcasted that today was all business.

He tried to respond in kind, but he couldn't stop his gaze from dropping to her lips. Couldn't keep his mind from revisiting the feel of those lips against his, the taste of her mouth as she'd kissed him. The sudden desire for a big glass of cabernet filled him.

When he dragged his gaze back to her eyes, they were slightly narrowed. The hands around her mug whitened at the knuckles. Her gaze drifted to his mug and then a smile quirked her lips. "Are you drinking chai?"

"Yeah."

That smile quivered again, making him wonder if he'd missed something, and then Keara cleared her throat, her expression turning serious.

"So there are no other bombs with this symbol?" she demanded. "Not anywhere in the country over the past seven years?"

Woof! Patches went to Keara and nudged her, making her reposition her mug to prevent her drink from spilling.

From the smell that wafted toward him, she'd opted for hot chocolate. He tried not to wonder what that would taste like on her lips.

"Sorry, Patches," Keara said, taking a seat and petting his dog.

Finally, she turned back to him with raised eyebrows.

"No. And when it comes to bombs, since the FBI has the biggest lab in the country dedicated to bomb evidence, we probably would have seen it. Unless—"

"Unless the other bombs exploding destroyed the symbols," Keara finished for him. "Maybe we were never intended to see that symbol at all. Maybe that's why Rodney had to kill Juan, because even if Rodney didn't kill Celia, the crime was now connected to the symbol."

"Killing Juan doesn't change the case file," Jax reminded her.

"No. But Juan was the only one showing any interest in Rodney," Keara shot back, her expression as desperate as it was determined.

Jax stared at her, dread sinking to his stomach. This tenuous connection between the murder in

Texas and the bomb had reignited Keara's hope that her husband's case could be solved. Based on the way she'd responded to the symbol the first time she'd seen it, that was something she'd given up on until now.

This new chance could be making her see connections where there weren't any. Was his hope that she could move on making him do the same?

If so, were they both fooling themselves that they could possibly solve Juan's cold case?

SHE NEEDED TO keep her distance from Jax.

Maybe not physically, since he was helping her investigate the bombing—and hopefully her husband's murder. That was giving her access to information she'd never be able to get from the FBI otherwise. So simply staying away from him wasn't an option. But separating herself emotionally was.

Sighing, Keara signed another document in the huge stack of paperwork on her desk and set it in her outbox. Being chief, even in a small town, meant a lot of paperwork. It had taken her several years to get used to the amount of time she spent at her desk, rather than out in the field. A small town in a place like Alaska—with more than twenty percent as much land as the whole of the lower forty-eight, but the lowest population density anywhere in the country—meant she still had to take calls personally. That fact had made the transition easier.

Slowly, she'd gotten used to being the boss. Of maintaining a certain distance between herself and her colleagues. Of being tougher on her officers than she would have wanted in their place, because she knew how important it was not just to maintain her authority, but also to keep them safe.

It wasn't easy. Not just the loss of the camaraderie she'd had when she was just one of the force, but also being hard on her officers. She'd even fired one, a rookie who'd had tons of promise and she'd liked personally, too. But he'd ignored direct orders, actually broken the law. Yes, he'd done it to save someone, and in his place, she might have done the same. But that didn't matter. Not now.

She had to do whatever it took to make sure none of her officers' spouses ever faced what she'd experienced. It was a responsibility that weighed heavily on her every day.

Still, most days she loved being a chief in Desparre. She loved the way a town known for its self-sufficient, independent citizens would pull together and look after each other when needed. And she was proud of the officers who worked for her, proud to call herself their chief.

There were definitely days when she missed being a detective. Missed working closely with a partner, unraveling a puzzle to give someone justice. She'd made the conscious choice to put that role behind her after Juan's death had gone unsolved. But now…

She shook her head and pushed her chair back from her desk, then stood and stretched. She'd been dealing with paperwork for hours, ever since she'd left The Lodge.

Coffee with Jax and Patches had felt more like a date than a professional meeting, despite the fact that they'd only talked about the case. Her fingers pressed against her lips, remembering the feel of his kiss, wishing she could get it out of her head.

She hadn't dated since Juan had died. Not really. Sure, she'd gone on a few "you'd get along so well; what's the big deal; give it a try" kind of setup dates. The kind where she'd met a guy for a drink, tried not to feel uncomfortable as he asked her what it was like being new to Alaska, what it was like being a police chief, then finally gone home. A couple of times, the guy had called for a second date and she'd let him down easy.

She'd told herself it was just too awkward to date in a town where she was the top law-enforcement official. She'd told herself that one day this would feel more like home and the timing would be better. But maybe that was an easy excuse. Because somehow, here it was, six years later, and Desparre *did* feel like her home. Yet, she hadn't gone out on a single date since those early setups.

Maybe it was pure bad luck, because she'd also never felt a connection to anyone like she'd been feeling with Jax over these past few days. At least, not since her husband.

The thought made her fingers drop away from her mouth and her stomach cramp up. Why did the first man who'd made her think about moving forward have to be one who was also forcing her to face her past?

Spinning away from the glass wall that gave her a view into the bullpen where some of her officers were working, Keara stared through the small window at the back of her office. The view was relaxing, the edge of a dense forest that butted up against this part of town. On the rare occasions that she opened the window, it filled her office with the chirping of birds and occasionally the call of a wolf. Once, she'd spotted a bear off in the distance.

When she'd first walked into this office, knowing it was going to be hers, she'd felt like she could breathe deeply for the first time in a year. Alaska had given her solace, a place to start over and hopefully, to heal.

Now, for the first time, she wondered if her family was right. Maybe she wasn't here to move on. Maybe she was here to escape the constant reminders that had been everywhere in Houston. The home she'd shared with Juan, their favorite restaurant, the streets they'd once patrolled together. Even the shared friends, the family who meant well but cringed and didn't quite meet her gaze when someone mentioned Juan's name.

Being in Houston, knowing Juan's killer was out there somewhere, walking free while Juan was gone, had filled her with a constant rage on top of the grief. And then there'd been the weight of failure, the knowledge that she—a police officer, a *detective*—hadn't been able to get Juan justice.

Coming here had made it all fade into the background. But it was returning now, that familiar weight that seemed to suffocate her from the inside.

She couldn't run forever. Maybe the bombing wasn't connected to Juan's murder. But whether it was the key or not, regardless of the fact that she had no jurisdiction, she was going to investigate.

The thought made the grief and anger and frustration burning inside her coalesce into something more powerful. Determination.

Keara glanced at the picture she kept framed in a corner of her office, almost hidden behind stacks of paper. Juan stared back at her, serious and proud in his police uniform from when they'd first started dating.

"I promise you," she whispered to that picture, her voice cracking, "this time I'm not giving up. I'm not running away. I'm going to figure out who killed you."

Chapter Nine

"Has there been *any* progress in the FBI's investigation? Are we any closer to knowing who did this?"

Justin Peterson's questions were full of frustration, but far less anger than when Jax and Patches had last visited the man. Maybe that was because today the visit was in his home, instead of the hospital.

"Absolutely," Jax said, leaning forward even as Patches continued to do her work.

She'd sat beside Justin as soon as the man led them into his living room. He'd been absently petting her ever since. His three-year-old daughter, Lily, was sprawled on the floor, chatting nonsense to Patches.

Every few minutes Patches would suddenly drop to her belly, full of puppy energy, and Lily would burst into giggles and pet her.

"What is it?" Justin asked, but this time he cracked a smile as Patches did more of her antics and Lily laughed again.

"I know it seems like a slow process, but doing it the right way now means we won't damage evidence that might help us later. It means that we're checking everything carefully so we get the person responsible. And we will. The FBI has a lot of experience with this kind of crime. And the lead agent managing this case, Agent Nez, has investigated a lot of bombings in his career."

Justin nodded slowly, finally seeming to believe the words Jax had been repeating for five days now. "Someone should pay for this."

His gaze dropped to his leg. He'd pulled up the fabric of his pants on his right side to show Jax before Lily had come into the room. A nasty scar traveled all the way from his ankle to his knee, where doctors had dealt with the large piece of metal that had been lodged there. "It ain't pretty. But at least they saved my leg. At least I'm still here."

Tears filled his eyes that he quickly swiped away as he glanced at his daughter, oblivious as she rolled over and Patches did the same.

A laugh burst free and Justin muttered, "Maybe we need to think about getting a dog."

"Yes, Daddy!" Lily screeched, leaping up and throwing her arms around Patches's neck. "A dog like Patches!"

Woof! Patches jumped to her feet, too.

"Better ask your mom," Justin said and Lily went racing out of the room. "Careful!" Justin called after her.

"We'll continue to be in touch," Jax said, shaking the man's hand as he stood. "I'm glad you're home. I'll keep you updated about the progress. And you can call me if you have questions."

"I appreciate it." A genuine smile lit Justin's face as his daughter screeched from the other room, "Mommy said yes!"

"Good luck," Jax said, then turned to his dog, who was staring in the direction Lily had disappeared. "Come on, Patches."

She followed him out the door and Jax felt his own smile break free. He was helping these victims. Slowly, but surely, they were all starting to move forward. Some were taking smaller steps than others and some had much harder journeys, but they'd all get there.

It was why he'd made the jump to the FBI. He was good at this. Maybe Ben and Anderson were right. Maybe he needed to stick to what he knew best, his own job.

As much as he wanted to help Keara, as much as he wanted to be more directly involved in stopping the person responsible, everything that was emerging from the FBI investigation suggested his and Keara's theories were off base.

There were no other bombs with the symbol. It was possible, though unlikely, that this was the only time the bomber had used the symbol. A bit more likely was that it had only been recovered in this particular bomb. But when Jax had floated that idea with Ben, the agent had seemed unconvinced. More likely, this guy was solely a bomber and the murder in Texas was unrelated. It was what Ben and Anderson believed. They even questioned if the symbols really matched. The loops were so random, they wondered if it was just coincidence, and that Keara, desperate to find connections to the old murders, was seeing what she wanted to see.

And yet… Jax couldn't shake the feeling he'd had when he'd first seen that symbol, the certainty that it meant something. He couldn't shake the memory of Keara's eyes widening, the way she'd swayed and gone pale, when she'd seen it.

Once he and Patches climbed into his SUV, Jax didn't bother to start the engine. Instead, he pulled out his cell phone and dialed Ben.

"Ben Nez," the agent answered. Even over the phone, he sounded commanding, the tone of someone who'd been an agent for a long time and was comfortable being in control.

"It's Jax. I'm just leaving one of the victim's houses and I have a question."

"A question or information on the case?" Ben asked, a warning tone in his voice, like he knew what was coming.

Ignoring it, Jax pushed forward. He could take the snide comments about being a wannabe agent. What he couldn't take was worrying that he'd kept quiet when speaking up might have made a difference. "I'm just wondering if we have any more details on the bomb. You've got a lot of experience with weapons like this. Does it seem like it's the work of someone who's been doing it a long time? Do you think whoever did this has made bombs before?"

A heavy sigh, meant to be heard, greeted him, followed by a long silence.

Finally, Jax broke it. "This isn't idle curiosity. What do you think?"

"It's hard to say," Ben said, his tone cautious. "The bomb itself wasn't very sophisticated. You can learn how to make something like this on the internet if you know where to look. But the fact that no one noticed anything unusual, that we don't have any cameras that caught anything suspicious, suggests this guy isn't an amateur. Plus, we've been looking hard for a motive, since the most likely reason to target this location is to take out a specific person. So far we haven't come up with anything promising."

"So—"

"You're a great Victim Specialist, Jax," Ben said, cutting him off. "And if there's information you're getting from the victims that could help us figure this out, I want to hear it. If you're asking about this because it's going to somehow help you in your role, then fine. But being an investigator isn't something you do off the side of your desk, no matter what you might have seen on TV."

Jax stiffened. He'd worked side by side with Special Agents and other members of the FBI for four years. He understood all too well how many people—agents, evidence technicians, victim specialists, analysts and more—came together to solve a crime.

"I know I'm not an agent," Jax said, wishing the words didn't feel just a little bit bitter. "And I'm not trying to be one." That much was true. Despite the burnout he was feeling, despite the desire to be more embedded in the investigative side of things, he did love his job. "But this case is different. This case—"

"This isn't the first time you've stepped outside your lines," Ben contradicted. "I don't know if this is how things ran when you were on the Rapid Deployment Team…"

"Not really," Jax admitted. Yes, he'd shared his insights when he could, but he'd often worked with big task forces. And his time at a particular crime scene had been very focused.

Alaska was different. The field office was big, but so was the area they covered. When he'd had psychological insight into a case, the agents had listened. To be fair, that had always included Ben.

Maybe he was stepping over the line with this case. Thinking of his clandestine meeting with Keara just that afternoon, Jax mentally crossed off the *maybe*.

"I'm sorry," Jax said. "You're right. It's just that the symbol is really bothering me in this case."

"We're looking into it," Ben said, but his tone told Jax the truth.

They'd already decided it wasn't important.

"I'm not an agent," Jax said again, sitting up straighter and making Patches stick her nose between the seats.

Absently petting her, Jax insisted, "And I'm not a profiler, either. But my background is in psychology. That means I understand a lot about human motivation and people's desires, especially the ones they can't seem to help. All of my training, all of my experience, is telling me there's something to this symbol."

There was another pause, but this one was shorter. "Fair enough," Ben said. "Do you know what?"

"No. But the fact that you haven't been able to connect it to anything else? The fact that this strange symbol was also near a murder? There's something here."

He'd been trying to deny it, but he couldn't shake the gut feeling he'd had from the beginning. "I need a favor."

"Okay," Ben said, reluctance in his tone, but less hostility.

"Run the symbol through the FBI's database again. This time do it without the bomb specification. See if that symbol has appeared at the scene of any other type of crime."

"I'll do it," Ben said, "but look, I've been down this kind of rabbit hole before, trying to make connections that aren't there. Be prepared for disappointment."

It had been six long years since she'd been embedded in a case like a detective, sorting through the evidence and clues. But sitting in her relaxing Alaskan home—her escape—with her laptop open to two case files and a mug of coffee that had long since gone cold, a familiar buzz filled Keara.

She loved being a police chief. She liked and respected all of the officers on her force and admired the spirit of the people of Desparre. Moving here had done so much for her mental health. It had made her feel like she was allowed to have a life again, that it wasn't a betrayal to keep living it, without Juan.

For the most part she hadn't really missed being a detective. That role came with too many memories. The surprise party Juan had thrown her when she passed her detective's exam and got promoted. The initial thrill of working a desk in the bullpen close to him. Working as partners had been against policy, since they'd just gotten married when she was promoted. But seeing him across the detectives' area each day had reminded her of their early times together, patrolling.

She'd expected being a detective would bring them closer, feel more like it had at the beginning, when they'd worked together every day. But too quickly, discussions about their cases had started interfering with their relationship. Most of it had been subtle, like the slow deterioration of their romantic dinners into sharing case files over takeout.

Then there'd been the expectations Keara had never seen coming. Being a patrol officer was dangerous, in Juan's opinion. But with Keara in a detective's seat, he'd wanted to try and have kids immediately. While she'd been working late to fit in—being a detective was still a bit of a boys' club—he'd been imagining babies. Toward the end of his life, when Keara thought they had plenty of time to figure it out, they'd started fighting over what they wanted, and when. Now it was all too late.

She minimized the case file for her husband's murder that Fitz had sent her unofficially. It hadn't been easy to go through, though thankfully, Fitz had left out the crime scene photos.

Seven years had dulled some of her grief, taken it from a sharp-edged pain that made it hard to breathe to something duller and more manageable. But she couldn't help wondering if things might have turned out differently if she and Juan hadn't made a pact to stop talking business and focus more on their relationship in those last six months. Would she have seen the threat coming? Would she have been able to prevent it?

"You can't change the past." Keara repeated the words her police-employed psychiatrist had told her seven years ago, when she wasn't ready to hear them. "You can only impact what happens in your future."

Ironic that more and more, the key to moving on seemed like it would involve revisiting her past.

And yet, was it too late? Seven years was a long time in the investigative world. There was a reason those cases were considered cold. A reason they were set aside and detectives' time reallocated to newer cases. A reason they were rarely reopened, unless some new evidence suddenly came to light.

Rubbing the back of her head, where a headache had started to form, Keara skimmed through Juan's interview with Rodney Brown one more time. The notes were slim, the interview itself a long-shot possibility. No matter how many times Keara reread them, she didn't see anything now that her husband hadn't seen back then. Except...

Keara jerked forward, yanking her laptop closer as an offhand mention describing Rodney's house caught her eye. "Lives with a roommate, not home," Juan had written.

Juan had originally gone to interview Rodney thinking he might have seen something relevant since his car had been photographed near the crime scene the night Celia Harris was killed. Although it was good police work not to rule anyone out as a suspect too quickly, Rodney hadn't been considered one initially. The only reason

Juan had left that interview with even mild suspicion was that Rodney had denied driving his car anywhere near the crime scene.

Happening to be near a crime scene wasn't a crime. Still, Juan had thought it was more likely Rodney was just afraid of police after his various assault arrests rather than a legitimate suspect, especially since he had no apparent connection to Celia. While the assault charges and the probable sexual assault told them he wasn't a nice guy, the specifics didn't suggest possible serial killer.

Like hundreds of other people who'd been interviewed in the Celia Harris murder, Rodney Brown had been pushed to the bottom of the list of people who might know something. But what if Juan had been approaching it from the wrong angle?

What if the reason Rodney had so vehemently insisted he hadn't been driving anywhere near the crime scene that night was because he hadn't? What if the roommate had used his car?

A thrill ran through Keara, a jolt of adrenaline she hadn't felt in a long time—the gut feeling that she was onto something with a case.

When Rodney had disappeared, the follow-up interview by Fitz said the house had been cleared out. So that meant the roommate had disappeared, too. Had they left together? Had they been in on Celia's murder together?

Or maybe her earlier theory had been right

all along. Maybe the person who'd set the bomb had intentionally used the symbol from Celia's murder to throw suspicion on someone else—his roommate.

If she was right, that triggered a lot of new questions: Who had killed Celia and who had set the bomb? Which of those two had killed her husband, Rodney or his roommate?

And where were they both now?

Chapter Ten

Every officer in the Desparre police station turned to stare at Jax as he strode through the station, following Officer Tate Emory to Keara's office.

Jax tried not to feel self-conscious as he juggled two cups of takeout coffee, wondering why he was getting so much attention. He'd been here before; it wasn't like the officers didn't know who he was. Maybe it was the overstuffed bag he had slung over one shoulder, full of FBI case printouts Ben had handed him that morning. Or maybe they could read his newly cautious hope about what those printouts might contain.

As Jax gave subdued nods of greeting to the officers who met his gaze, Patches bounded around him, occasionally darting to a desk for a pat from one of the officers before running back to his side.

"What's going on?" Jax asked Tate softly.

Tate's gaze briefly scanned the room before coming back to him. "Something's up with the chief," he said, then knocked on the door to Keara's office before pushing it open.

From across the station's bullpen, through the glass walls into her office, Keara had merely appeared hard at work. From a distance, he'd assumed her normal professional face was on. It was calm and serious and confident, probably something that had helped her win Desparre's trust when she'd first shown up here, an outsider and young for a police chief job.

Jax had known from her frantic call at seven that morning—when he and Patches had barely been awake—that she was reenergized about the bombing investigation and its possible connection to Juan's death. He should have realized this new information about a roommate she'd discovered would only fuel Keara's desperation.

Up close, he could see the dark circles underneath her eyes that suggested she'd been awake long before she'd called him, maybe that she hadn't gone to bed at all. Jittery energy radiated from her.

As he stepped more fully into the room, she stood and reached for one of the coffees he held. "Is this for me?"

"Yes," he answered.

Woof! Patches circled Keara, tail wagging.

"Easy, Patches," Jax warned her, not wanting his dog to trip Keara.

"She's fine," Keara said, bending down to pet Patches and getting rewarded by a dog kiss across her cheek. Keara laughed, then took a long sip of coffee, closing her eyes like she'd badly needed the caffeine jolt.

Tate gave Jax a raised-eyebrow look that

seemed to say "See what I mean?" before he left the office, closing the door behind him.

Jax took a minute to watch Keara while she had her eyes closed, exhaustion and hope battling on her face. All the while, she pet Patches.

His dog's tail wagged, but she glanced back at him, as if she also wondered what was going on with Keara.

What must it be like to have spent seven years knowing someone she loved had been murdered and not being able to do anything about it? What must it be like now, to have this sudden, long-shot hope again?

Dread tightened his chest, knowing he was partly responsible. If they were both wrong, how much worse would it be for Keara?

Her eyes opened, her gaze instantly locking on his like she'd read his thoughts. Instead of making him feel more guilty, the intensity there made his own hope ignite.

What if they were right? What if they could solve her husband's murder? What if she was finally able to get closure and move on with her life? He lived too far away to be a part of it in any meaningful way, but knowing that didn't stop a sudden longing.

She broke eye contact, standing, and her tone was all business when she said, "Let's get to work."

He'd spent the morning like he had almost

every other morning since he'd arrived in Luna, talking to victims and their families. Today he'd mostly been returning personal effects. For some of the victims, it was a welcome visit, a sign of moving forward. For others, it was a stark reminder of what, or who, they'd lost.

At lunchtime, when his mind had been ping-ponging between the idea of Rodney Brown having a roommate and the needs of the bombing victims, Ben had asked to meet. He'd handed over a stack of printouts and told Jax, "This is your theory, so I'm going to let you run with it. It's not protocol and I'm definitely going to be reviewing all of this myself as soon as I get a chance, but I'm expecting you to return the favor. You find something—anything at all—and I want to be your first call. Deal?"

Jax had looked down at the massive stack of printouts, then back at Ben, who'd grinned and said, "Our databases aren't magic. I input the details of the symbol, but with parameters this wide—connected to any crime over the past seven years—it spit out a *lot* of cases across the country. There's a good chance none of them are connected to the bombing or the murder, because the system matches descriptions. And it's all different law enforcement entering them, not just FBI. It's you who has to pull up the actual pictures and do a visual comparison. Still…"

"There's a chance," Jax had said. "It's a deal.

I'll call you if I find anything," he'd agreed, although the first thing he'd done when Ben left the room was call Keara and let her know he was coming to the station and needed her help. He knew Ben had thrown the material at him because he still felt doubtful about a connection to the symbol and was more than willing to let Jax do the heavy lifting on that aspect of the case.

"Let's see the cases," she said.

"There are a lot," he warned, pulling out the massive pile of paperwork. "The database spits out all possibilities. It's up to us to wade through them all and narrow it down."

She gave him a one-sided grin and held her coffee cup up like she was making a toast. "Welcome to the life of a detective, Jax. Let's take a look."

As she cleared off some space on her desk and gestured for him to take the seat across from her chair, she asked, "Does the FBI know I'm helping you with this?"

"No." He settled into the seat and set half the stack in front of him, passing her the other half.

Instead of sitting beside him, Patches followed Keara around to her side of the desk.

As Keara dug into her stack of files, Jax couldn't help but stare at her carefully tied-back hair and light, professional makeup. Even the first day he'd met her, dressed down in jeans and a raincoat, she'd looked like someone who was in charge. But the day he'd stopped by her house unannounced…

He smiled at the memory of her hair spilling over her shoulders, the cabernet staining her lips like a funky lipstick. It was a look he doubted many people in Desparre got to see, even on her days off.

"Stop staring and start reading," Keara said, without glancing up.

The smile grew and he held in a laugh. Why couldn't he have met her under different circumstances? Without her husband's unsolved murder hanging over her head like a dark cloud? Without four hundred miles between their homes?

As his smile faded, he asked, "Any luck finding the roommate?"

Her gaze met his, serious and determined. A look that said she would search as long as it took. "No. Assuming Juan was right, this guy wasn't listed on the lease with Rodney. I haven't been able to dig up so much as a name." Her lips tightened as she blew out a heavy breath. "Whoever he is, he's as much of a ghost as Rodney, maybe even more so."

As Jax stared at her, she broke eye contact, lines creasing her forehead. There was a hint of fear underneath her words as she said, "Seven years is a long time. I'm scared I won't be able to track him."

"We can do it," Jax said, resisting the urge to reach his hand out and take hers.

From the other side of the desk, Patches made a slight whining sound, her way of getting attention when she knew someone needed her but wasn't paying attention. From Keara's suddenly surprised look, Patches had also pushed her head into Keara's lap, insisting on being pet.

Some of the lines raking Keara's forehead disappeared as she pet Patches.

He said a silent *thank you* to his dog, then continued, "There is one piece of good news here."

She looked up at him again.

"If he's trying so hard to stay beneath the radar that you're struggling to even find mention of his name, there's probably a reason. We might really be onto our bomber."

"THERE HAS TO BE *something* here," Keara muttered as she set aside yet another case description in her *No* pile.

She and Jax had been sorting through the huge stack of cases he'd brought for almost an hour. In that time, Jax's stack of unrelated cases had grown almost as high as hers. They had a few *Maybe*s, but years spent as an officer, then a detective, then a police chief told Keara none of them were likely to be connected to the bombing, Celia's murder, or Juan's murder.

She'd been so hopeful when Jax had walked

into her office, carrying such a big stack of possibilities. After her sleepless night, having Jax to help—along with his calming presence and Patches's cute distraction—had made her feel like answers had to be in sight.

She wasn't so far removed from her time as a detective that she'd forgotten the slog of it all. The hours that felt unending and pointless until one small detail broke open a case. Both Juan's and Celia's cases had remained open for a year, with Houston detectives logging thousands of hours on them, and they still hadn't found that one detail.

Lately, Keara had spent too much time fighting a roller coaster of emotions, rocketing from a certainty she'd finally get closure to the fear that she'd get nowhere and just end up back where she'd been six years ago. Grief-ridden, brokenhearted and stuck.

Back then she'd reacted by finding a tiny job posting across the country, far from anyone she knew. Getting the job had been a surprise; when she'd taken it, her family and friends had all been shocked. Until five days ago, it had felt like a brand-new start.

"We've got a couple of possibilities," Jax reminded her, his dark brown eyes full of determination, like he was trying to lend her strength.

She gave him a shaky smile, both appreciating the effort and not wanting him to see too deeply into her soul. Working with detectives was hard enough—they were trained to see what you weren't telling them. But someone with years of experience as a psychologist and a therapist? The more time she spent with him, the more she wondered if he could tell everything she was thinking.

She redirected her gaze to her stack of cases before Jax could make out the other thing she couldn't help feeling when he was around—attraction.

He was so different from Juan. Half a foot taller, Jax was slower to smile but more likely to have it burst into a full-blown grin when he did. His skin was darker and smoother, his body more lean muscle than Juan's heavier bulk.

But it was more than just the physical differences. Her husband had been hard to win over, suspicious and wary until you proved you could be trusted. Jax seemed to approach everyone like his friend, until proven otherwise. Probably a result of their respective professions.

In other ways, she could see definite similarities. Juan could fill a conversation with lots of small talk so you didn't even realize you'd shared a lot more with him than he had with you. It was a skill that had come in handy as a detective, but frustrated her in the early stages of their relationship. Only once they'd been dating for a few years had he really started opening up to her.

From the little bit she'd asked about Jax's personal life, he hadn't seemed closed off at all. Still, he was good at pulling personal information out of others. It was certainly something that was helping him reach victims. Maybe that was why she'd connected so easily to him.

Was that all this was? Her projecting a connection because she needed someone to help her process the fact that Juan's death had gone unsolved? That she'd *let* it go unsolved, by running across the country instead of staying and trying to figure it out herself?

"No," Jax said and for a minute, Keara wondered if she'd spoken her thoughts out loud.

"What?"

He sighed, ran a hand through his hair that mussed it up just enough to make Keara long to fix it for him. "I thought maybe I'd found something, but I didn't."

He tossed the case summary printout on his *No* pile, then gave her an encouraging smile. "We're onto something. I can feel it." His eyes were already on the next case file as he muttered, "We just have to keep searching."

A smile pulled at her lips despite how discouraged she'd started to feel. For a minute she just watched him, then Patches nudging her leg made her refocus.

Petting the dog with one hand, Keara flipped open a new case file and her heart gave a hard *thump*. "No way," she breathed. She yanked the page closer to her face to scrutinize the scanned picture of a symbol. It looked eerily similar to the one found at the murder, down to the spray paint.

"What is it?"

Jax sounded distracted and Keara shook her paper at him, her excitement growing. "I think I found something. It's..." She shook her head, surprised at the crime. But there was no question that the symbol was the same. "It's an *arson* case. Unsolved, no promising suspects. It's from six years ago, in Oklahoma." She set the paper down. "Maybe that's why the detectives never found Rodney after Juan died. He'd already moved on to Oklahoma."

"Keara." Jax looked up at her, surprise and intensity in his gaze. "I've got something, too."

Her pulse jumped again as she leaned toward him across the desk, trying to see his case details. "Another fire?"

"No, another murder. Five years ago, in Nebraska."

Excitement filled her, churning in her stomach along with too much coffee. "He was heading north. He was slowly moving toward Alaska."

Jax's gaze met hers again and she saw her excitement reflected there. "Maybe."

"Maybe? No, definitely." The buzz she'd felt last night when she'd discovered Rodney had a roommate returned, headier now.

She tossed the case information into her *Yes*

pile and kept searching. Over the next half hour, her excitement dimmed slightly, as no new cases looked connected. But then she and Jax found three more in rapid succession, until they had a stack of five with the exact same symbol. The symbol was drawn in different ways, found in different places at the crime scenes, but they had to be connected.

"We're onto him," Jax said, grinning at her over the newly divided stacks of cases.

The dimple just visible on his right cheek as he smiled at her almost made her smile back. Except...

"There's just one problem," Keara told him, dread already balling up in her stomach again.

"What? That we probably haven't found everything?" Jax referred to the fact that there was one time gap big enough that they'd agreed there was probably at least one more connected crime. "I'm sure another one will surface eventually."

"Not that," Keara said. "Every single one of these cases is in a different jurisdiction. Hell, every case is in a different *state*."

"Okay, but—"

"Jax, he set off this bomb in Luna, left behind this symbol." Frustration welled up, made her want to take it out at the gym on a punching bag. "This pattern suggests he commits one crime and then leaves. He's probably already gone."

He stared back at her, his grin slowly fading.

Beside her, Patches whined and nudged her leg.

Keara looked down at the dog and gave her a grateful smile, tried to will forward some positive energy. They'd found the criminal's trail, but had it already gone cold here?

Boom!

A sound like thunder directly overhead exploded in her ears, making her flinch and instinctively leap to her feet, her hand already near her weapon.

Through the glass walls of her office, her officers were doing the same, glancing questioningly at one another.

Then the silence following the loud noise was replaced by screaming.

Before Keara made it to her office door, the door into the bullpen opened.

Charlie Quinn, one of her longest-term veterans, appeared, looking pale. Even from a distance, she could read the words on his lips.

"Bomb."

Chapter Eleven

There was chaos in her police station.

Her officers were all racing for the door, some grabbing weapons from desks and shoving them in holsters, others looking around with panic. The door into the bullpen was open—and probably the door to the station beyond that—so Keara could hear the panicked cacophony outside, too. Screams, crying and a persistent wailing that sent a chill through her entire body.

After yanking open the door to her office, Keara raced into the chaos and yelled, "Wait!"

Her officers stopped moving toward the exit, but their gazes still darted all around. Her veterans seemed filled with anxious determination, ready to find out what was happening and help. Some of the newer officers looked stiff with uncertainty. None of them had ever faced anything like this.

Neither had she.

Dread settled in her gut, her pulse picking up at the worry she wouldn't know how to manage this properly. Houston was a big city, but even there, she'd never been on the scene of a bomb. The closest she'd come was seeing the aftermath of the Luna explosion.

"Right now we don't know anything."

"We know it was a bomb outside, maybe on the street," Charlie interrupted, his voice deeper than usual with tension. "Lorenzo and the Rook are out there."

At his words, everyone started moving again.

"Stop!" Keara demanded. "Listen. We need to be careful. What we don't know is if there are more bombs set. Sam, I need you to stay here and manage the station. Field calls, deal with anyone who comes in off the street and get paramedics on scene. Then call the hospital in Luna and tell them to expect injured. We might need their medevac helicopter. Line it up."

Sam Jennings nodded. He was a five-year veteran who was typically cool under pressure and great at multitasking, especially when it involved tech. But his movements were shaky as he headed toward the front of the station.

"Everyone else, keep your eyes open and stay in contact with each other. Let's go."

As her officers started running for the door, Keara turned back toward her office to ask Jax to inform the FBI.

He met her gaze immediately, and there was worry in his eyes, even as his attention seemed to be half on the phone at his ear. Moving the mouthpiece backward, he called to her, "I'm on with Anderson. The FBI is on the way. They're coming with agents and evidence techs. They'll handle the bigger investigation—they assume it's connected to Luna. They want you to focus on helping the injured and securing the scene."

Keara didn't bother being offended at the FBI instantly calling jurisdiction. They had more experience, more resources. She was happy to focus on the safety of her citizens and let the FBI take the lead. Nodding, Keara delayed a few seconds to take in the calm steadiness of Jax's presence. Then she took a deep breath and raced after her officers.

As soon as she stepped outside, a wisp of smoke wafted toward her, the acrid taste of it filling her mouth and then her lungs. Her eyes watered, partly from the smoke, but mostly from the scene in front of her.

The grassy park down the street from the police station—a popular place for citizens to dog walk or picnic—was now a bomb site. Flames leaped out from a small gazebo at the back of the park, close to the woods. The charred ground around it, a blackened patch where bright blue wild irises had just been starting to bloom, reminded her of the scene at Luna. The set of swings at the center of the park were warped and partially collapsed, one swing completely missing. People were scattered around, some lying on the ground, some hunched over, and others stumbling away.

She'd known some of the victims at the Luna bombing. She knew almost everyone who lived in Desparre.

Keara ran faster. She heard the heavy police station door slam closed and looked back to see Jax hurrying after her. She immediately glanced toward the ground at his side, but he'd left Patches in the station. Probably because of the debris that might be dangerous for her to walk on.

Whipping her gaze back to the park, Keara scanned the area, trying to take in everything at once. There were people staggering backward, their movements and expressions full of shock. Others seemed frozen. Still others were helping, moving toward the park instead of away from it, risking their own safety for their neighbors. That included her officers.

Whoever had done this was either fearless or making a statement. The park was less than a hundred feet from the police station.

Slowing to a stop as she neared the park, Keara searched for anyone whose reaction seemed out of place. Either too calm or worse, pleased. But everyone appeared shocked and scared. No one was hurrying away from the scene, either.

She glanced at Jax, who'd paused next to her. His expression was serious and troubled, but he still managed to radiate a certain calm. No wonder people gravitated toward him in a crisis.

He shook his head at her and she realized he'd been looking for the same thing, studying people with a psychologist's perspective.

Whoever the bomber was, he was either long gone or one hell of an actor.

"Chief!"

At the tearful tone of Lorenzo, one of her steadiest veterans, Keara's gaze whipped back to the park.

At the edge of the grassy area, near the road, Lorenzo was bent over someone.

The dread in her gut intensified, bubbling up a familiar grief. She didn't need to see the face of the person on the ground to know who it was. The newest and youngest member of her force. Lorenzo's partner, twenty-year-old Nate Dreymond.

Rushing over, Keara dropped to the grass next to Lorenzo.

Nate was prone on the ground, eyes closed and face ashen. There was blood on his head, and his arm was stretched out at an unnatural angle.

"We were heading out for patrol. Someone in the park called us over. I'm not sure who it was or what they wanted." Lorenzo's words were rapid-fire, his voice shaky. "Rook was ahead of me. When the bomb went off, something flew this way and slammed into him. I don't know what it's from, but—" he gestured to a piece of metal, twisted and unidentifiable, and covered in blood "—the force of the blast knocked me down, too." His hand, shaking violently, went to his own head.

When he met her gaze, his focus seemed off, too. "When I could get up, I came over here, but—"

"No," Keara whispered, the image of another man's blood filling her mind. She leaned down, pressing her ear to Nate's chest. She expected to hear nothing, but a weak *thump thump* came through.

"He's in bad shape," Lorenzo finished.

Letting out a long breath, Keara sat up again and barked into her radio, "Sam, get that medevac from the Luna hospital. Nate needs it."

She scanned his prone form, looking for injuries that needed immediate attention. She'd gotten basic training in first aid over the years in Houston. It had been a long time, though, and she frantically ran through the mental checklist she used to know by heart.

She didn't see any way to help him. He was unconscious with a clearly broken arm, but the blood on his head wasn't still flowing.

"Medevac is coming," Sam's strained voice informed her. "They're twenty minutes out."

"Help!"

Keara's head popped up at the cry. She put her hand on Lorenzo's arm and asked, "You okay?"

"Fine," Lorenzo said.

There was no doubt he needed to get checked out by a doctor, but she nodded. "Stay with Nate. Call me if anything changes."

Then she pushed to her feet and hurried

across the park to the person calling. The grass felt strange beneath her boots, crunchy where it should have been soft. As she ran, she passed by other Desparre citizens, some simply looking dazed and others clearly injured.

There was a family, fairly new to Desparre, with a six-year-old and a new baby on the way, hugging each other and crying. The owner of Desparre's downtown bar, wrapping his bleeding arm with his own shirt. A loner who lived up the mountain and came into the park every few weeks but still stuck with his own company, sat on the ground, looking dazed. He had a hand to his head and both legs were bleeding, but nothing was gushing.

Keara scanned each of them, but kept moving. None needed immediate attention.

The fire at the gazebo was growing, flames devouring most of it now. The structure was relatively far from other buildings, but it was close enough to the woods to be a concern. She lifted her radio and said, "We need to manage this fire."

"On it," Tate Emory answered and from her peripheral vision, she could see he was also on his cell phone, probably with the tiny fire department. They were located on the edge of Desparre and they served the whole county, including Luna and other neighboring towns. They were also all volunteer and had similar hours as her officers.

"I've got some citizens lined up to bring buckets from the bar while we wait for the fire department," Tate told her. "We should be able to keep this from jumping."

"Good. Radio if you need more help," she instructed, then jammed her radio back into her belt.

At the edge of the gazebo, she discovered who had called for help. Talise Poitra owned the grocery store in downtown Desparre. She was friendly and quick to advise outsiders, which Keara had discovered her first week in town. Talise had celebrated her seventieth birthday last month and hung balloons all over the grocery store. She'd stopped by the police station with cake and told them she insisted the entire town celebrate with her.

Right now the woman with the long gray hair, easy smile and deeply weathered skin from a lifetime in Alaska was holding her leg with one hand and her ear with the other. A deep gash ran the length of her right thigh and blood spurted out at regular intervals.

Swearing, Keara yanked at the sleeve of her police uniform until the arm ripped off. She dropped to her knees and tied the fabric around the top of Talise's leg. But no matter how hard she yanked the knot, blood was still pumping.

"I got it," Jax said, suddenly beside her, his belt in hand. "Brace yourself," he told Talise, then tightened the belt over the fabric.

Talise went pale, her eyes rolling backward as she swayed. But she stiffened before Keara could grab her. Her hands dropped to the ground, bracing herself, and Keara saw more blood on the woman's right ear.

Fury overlaid the dread she'd been feeling. This was *her* town. These people were *her* responsibility.

She put her hand on Talise's arm, trying to comfort her, even as her gaze met Jax's.

"Two bombs," he said, his tone filled with meaning she didn't understand.

She shook her head and he added, "Two bombs in less than a week. Just one town apart."

The implications sank in fast. The crimes they'd been poring over this afternoon had been filled with differences. The only commonality they'd shared besides the symbol was that the perpetrator hadn't struck again in the same jurisdiction, or even the same state.

"It's not the same person," she breathed.

Chapter Twelve

The day had gone by in a blur of blood and fire and pained cries. But rushing from one person to the next hadn't been able to fully distract him from the panic.

Over his years on the Rapid Deployment Team, he'd gotten used to mass casualty events. They didn't get any easier, but the fear and panic of his first few scenes hadn't returned in years. Not until today.

Only after most of the victims had been checked by paramedics and Keara was helping put out the last of the fire had he realized why. A flame had sparked, creating a loud *boom* that sounded like a bullet, and his gaze had leaped immediately to Keara.

In that moment it hit him. He was worried about her safety. He was worried about *her*.

Recognizing where the panic was coming from created a different kind of worry, but he'd pushed it aside and spent the rest of the day focusing on the victims.

Jax was exhausted. So was Patches, who'd joined him at the scene as soon as it was clear enough to be safe. The two of them had talked to as many victims as possible. They'd also spent time comforting the Desparre officers, who had never seen anything like this.

For all of his exhaustion, the people around him were even more tired. Ben and Anderson coming in with their FBI team had taken the weight of the investigation off the Desparre PD, but it hadn't taken away the responsibility.

He could see it as he eyed Keara from his peripheral vision, trudging beside him, leaving the bomb site. There was soot smeared across her forehead, someone else's blood on her arms and a furious determination on her face.

As she glanced back at the scene, barely visible in the moonlight, he told her, "There's nothing else you can do there tonight."

Walking between them, Patches nudged Keara with her nose, always sensitive to people's needs.

Keara smiled fondly down at his dog, petting her head as she refocused on their destination: the police station.

Anderson jogged up beside them, shivering even with his FBI jacket zipped all the way up. The agent had come from Los Angeles and even after being in Alaska longer than Jax, he still hadn't acclimated. His normally perfect hair was sticking up in all directions and there were dark craters under his eyes. "We'll be taking another look at that symbol now that we've seen it at a second bomb site."

Jax felt his heart thump harder. "It was on this bomb, too?"

"Not on the bomb. We found it on a tree behind the gazebo. It was carved there, pretty recently, judging by the state of it."

Keara frowned, looking more perplexed than encouraged by the news.

Anderson glanced from Jax to Keara and back again. "Ben said you were combing through other crimes that might have the same symbol. Any luck?"

Jax gave a frustrated shrug. "We thought so, but now I'm not so sure they match. I'll flag them for you guys to look, but…"

"Seems like more than one person is using the same symbol," Anderson finished, not sounding surprised.

Jax glanced at Keara, wanting her take on it, and she gave a discouraged nod.

"This symbol means something we don't understand yet," Anderson said. "You were right about that, Jax. Whatever the meaning, it sounds like it's important to more than one criminal. Maybe it's connected to an organization, possibly some kind of underground group."

"But *what*?" Keara muttered. "The Houston PD researched it seven years ago. *I* researched it this week. None of us came up with anything."

Anderson shrugged, covering a yawn with his hand. "Or it could be more personal. Maybe we have a couple of criminals who were a team once and now they're both taking the symbol to their own crimes."

Keara's troubled gaze met his and he could practically read her thoughts: *If the symbol was from some personal event, how would they ever figure it out?*

Patches nudged her again as they reached the police station and Keara pet her once more before holding open the door.

Jax filed inside with Patches, but Keara stayed there, holding the door open and thanking each of her exhausted officers—and all of the FBI agents, too—as they walked past her.

She was a good chief. It couldn't have been easy for her, being the only woman on the force, being so young for her role and being an outsider, too. But it was obvious her officers respected her. Despite how personally each of them had been touched by today's tragedy, they mustered up weak nods for her in return.

Even the FBI agents, who could sometimes get frustrated with small-town officers who had little experience dealing with major crimes, seemed impressed by Keara and her team.

As Keara finally followed them inside, Sam stood up behind the front desk. "Any news on Nate?"

Keara swept her gaze over her officers, who had all stopped in the entryway of the station to listen. "The hospital is going to update us when there's any change. I'll keep you all informed."

Keara's youngest rookie had been in bad shape when the helicopter had lifted off. So had its other occupant, the grocery store owner who was far stronger than she looked to have held on until the medevac team arrived. Five other people had been taken to the hospital, too, but they'd gone by ambulance, taking the hour ride up and down the mountain to get to Luna. But at least—as of right now—no one had been killed in this bombing.

"We're going to relocate over to Desparre," Ben said, moving to the front of the crowd.

The seasoned agent, who'd lived in Alaska most of his life and managed other scenes where explosives had been set off, was holding up better than most of them. But even he had cracks in his stoicism, with a tight set to his jaw that suggested this case had him worried.

"There's a hotel just a few miles outside of town," Keara said. "It's called Royal Desparre. It's a nice place, but we don't get many tourists here. They'll have vacancies."

"Thanks," Ben said. "Let's go," he called to the other FBI agents and employees, and then he told Keara, "We'll be back in the morning."

As they trudged out of the station, Jax lagged behind. He didn't want to leave without a chance to talk to Keara alone. He wanted to see how she really felt about the new bombing and what they'd found this afternoon. But it was more than that. He also wanted to be able to talk to her outside her official capacity, away from people who relied on her to set the tone and be a leader. To make sure she was really okay.

"You coming?" Anderson called to him as Keara's officers all started heading out the door, too.

Jax looked at Keara and found her gaze already on him. "I have a pull-out couch," she said, loud enough for Anderson to hear. "In case they won't let Patches stay in the hotel."

Anderson didn't look like he bought her reasoning, but Jax jumped on it. "That would be great. Thanks."

Patches gave her own *woof* of approval.

Keara nodded stiffly at him, then turned away, checking on each of her officers individually. She made sure each one was able to drive home, then waited until they'd all left the station before she finally returned her attention to him.

"How are you holding up?" he asked.

Patches hurried over to her side again, sitting next to Keara and staring up at her. But it wasn't the look Patches gave when she was trying to help someone; this was his dog becoming attached.

Jax stared at Patches as Keara began to pet his dog, and new anxiety filled him. He was becoming attached to Keara, too. Whenever the end of this case came, he wasn't sure he was going to be ready to stop seeing her every day.

Keara pet Patches for a long moment without answering. Then her troubled gaze met his. "How do you do this, case after case?"

"What do you mean?"

"This." She gestured toward the front door. "How do you come to these scenes, tragedy after tragedy?" Her voice cracked as she continued, "How do you wade into them, again and again, hearing about the worst thing someone has experienced?"

He shrugged, gave her a small smile. "I'm good at it. Patches is good at it."

Woof!

Another smile broke free as he told her, "That's right, Patches." Then he said to Keara, "It's not easy. But knowing that I've helped someone makes it worthwhile. What about *you*?"

She laughed, but it was short and bitter. "The type of crime scene I've probably been called to most often in Desparre is a bar fight. This is way outside of my comfort zone. I didn't experience anything like this, even in Houston."

Jax flashed back to the dangerous situation in the Luna bar the day he'd met her. His arms were still healing from being sliced through with broken bottles when the drunk had yanked him off the bar. He could still feel the panic when he'd jumped into the fray, worried the mob of men was going to overrun Keara at any moment.

"I mean, how do you handle constantly running into danger?"

"It's part of the job. I accepted the danger a long time ago, when I took the oath to become a police officer. But I've been at this career since I was twenty-three. I still get scared on calls sometimes, but I trust my training and I trust my officers to have my back. And I believe in what I do. That's worth the fear."

She frowned, staring at the ground, her hand pausing on Patches's head. Her voice was almost a whisper when she admitted, "It's not the physical danger that really scares me. It's the cases I can't solve. That's what keeps me up at night."

When her gaze met his again, he saw years of pain reflected back at him. "What scares me is the idea that I'll never be able to solve Juan's murder. And that as long as it remains unsolved, I'll never be able to fully move forward myself."

KEARA WOKE UP disoriented, a headache pounding at her temples and the smell of smoke lodged in her nostrils. Against her back was a strong, warm body.

In a flash, the night before returned to her. Making the short drive from the police station to her house, every second stretching out as she'd fought to keep her eyes open. Jax in the seat beside her and Patches lightly snoring in the back.

When they'd finally pulled up to her house,

she'd barely had the energy to trade the uniform she'd worn to the crime scene for joggers and a long-sleeved T-shirt. She'd leaned over the sink and scrubbed her hands, face and arms, but sleep had sounded more appealing than a shower.

She'd returned to her living room to find Jax already changed into sweatpants and a T-shirt emblazoned with Fidelity. Bravery. Integrity. Apparently, he carried extra clothes everywhere he went.

In that moment, with the weight of the town's expectations and Juan's unsolved case, Jax— half a foot taller than she was with the body of a federal agent and the eyes of a therapist—had seemed like the perfect person to help her shoulder some of it. So when he'd walked over and put his arms around her, she'd sunk into his embrace.

She vaguely recalled him walking her over to the couch and coaxing her to lie down against him. As soon as she'd laid her head on his outstretched arm, the exhaustion had overcome her.

Despite the horror of the day before, despite the gnawing worry about her ability to solve Juan's case so many years later, it was the best she'd slept in years. She glanced at the floor below her, where Patches was just starting to stir, her feet twitching and her eyes opening.

When she met Keara's gaze, her tail started to thump against the wood floor and Keara whispered, "Shhh."

Nerves made her feel clumsy as she slowly slid forward on the couch, carefully lifting the arm draped over her waist. She barely breathed as she tried to slip away from Jax without waking him.

It had been seven long years since she'd woken up with a man's arm draped over her.

She finally took a deep breath as she sat up and Jax didn't move behind her. Carefully setting her feet down so she wouldn't step on Patches, she slid forward, hoping to stand without disturbing him.

"It's morning already?" Jax asked.

His voice was slightly deeper with sleep, and it sent a jolt of awareness through her, even as she cringed at having woken him.

"Yep," she said, her voice too cheery. She stood, heading toward the connected kitchen and resisting the urge to run a hand over her hair, which felt like a tangled mess, the bobby pins half out of her bun. "Coffee?"

Patches leaped up, racing after her, sliding as the planked wood floors of her living room gave way to slicker tile in the kitchen.

Keara couldn't stop the laugh that escaped as Patches ran around her in a circle, tail wagging. She looked more like a puppy than a therapy dog and Keara knew Patches was catching her nervous energy.

"Sounds good," Jax said from the living room. She could hear him standing, probably stretching, but she didn't glance back. Her neck and face felt warm with the knowledge that he knew exactly why she was trying to busy herself. It didn't take a psychology degree—which he had in multiples—to recognize that she was uncomfortable with what had happened between them last night. The fact that it had been a lot more innocent than the kisses they'd shared a few days ago didn't matter. Spending the night in his embrace had felt more intimate.

As she scooped coffee grinds into the machine, Jax joined her in the kitchen. From her peripheral vision, she saw him lean against her island and watch her.

Before she could get her scrambled brain to come up with small talk—or better yet, a coherent discussion about the investigation—he asked, "What did your family think about you moving across the country to be a police chief?"

"They weren't thrilled." She spun to face him and even knowing where he'd been standing, even though he was still a couple of feet away, it felt too close. His hair was slightly mussed from sleep, making her realize how curly it was, making her want to run her hands through it.

Fisting them at her sides, she continued, "But then, they kept hoping Juan's death would be a wake-up call that I needed to find another profession."

"They worry about you."

"Yeah. I'm an only child, but as my dad likes to joke, with Irish on one side and Italian on the other, we're not a small family. My aunt was a police officer and I was really close to her growing up. She worked a night shift during most of my childhood, and since my parents worked days, she'd pick me up from school every day. She was killed on the job the same year I got my badge."

"I'm sorry."

Keara nodded. The year her aunt had died had been the same time she'd been paired up with Juan. It had been a hugely bittersweet time in her life. She'd wanted to follow in her aunt's footsteps since she was a kid. She'd always imagined them working together someday.

"I've lived here for six years now and they still ask when I'm moving back on a pretty regular basis." She shrugged, even though it frustrated her. "At least it's coming from a place of love."

"What if we solve Juan's case?" Jax stared at her, his gaze so focused that even Patches quieted down.

Her heart jumped at the idea that he still thought it was possible. Jax wasn't an investigator, but over the past week, she'd discovered he made a great partner. "What do you mean?"

"If we solve it, would you consider moving back to Houston?"

She'd never thought about it. Moving to Alaska

had been a concession; her way of admitting that Juan's murder would always remain unsolved.

The Houston PD would probably take her back, if they had an opening. She'd had a good relationship with the officers and chief there. But what had started as a self-imposed exile and escape had become her home.

She shook her head. "I don't think so. I should visit more. I miss my family. But that was a different chapter of my life. Alaska is my future."

Saying the words out loud, she realized how true they were. It freed something inside her, made real happiness seem possible again. And staring at the Victim Specialist in her kitchen made even more seem possible.

Diverting her gaze before he read her thoughts, she spun back to the coffee machine, filled it with water and hit Brew.

When he didn't move, she turned back toward him, bracing her hands on the counter behind her. "This is my town, Jax." She sighed, the responsibilities crashing back around her. "I'm glad the FBI is taking lead in the new investigation. They have a lot more experience than I do. But when they leave, this will still be my home. These people will still be my responsibility. I'm officially involved now, so we don't need to be investigating on the side."

He pushed away from the island, his mouth opening.

She cut off the argument she could see coming. "That doesn't mean I want to stop working with you. I don't care what your title is. I want your psychological insight on this. But what we saw in the cases we dug up yesterday? They don't match what's happening here."

He frowned, lines creasing his forehead. "I know."

"If this were one person so savvy and determined to stay off police radar by jumping jurisdictions—hell, jumping *states*—between his crimes, why set off two bombs in less than a week? Most likely, this is still connected to the crimes we dug up *somehow*, if we can figure out that symbol. But right now we have a bigger problem."

Jax nodded. "We're looking at a serial bomber."

"Yeah. And with two bombs in six days, he's probably not finished."

Chapter Thirteen

Jax had a tendency to overanalyze things, but right now he knew exactly what he wanted.

He stared across the Desparre park at Keara, frowning as she talked to Ben and Anderson. As if she sensed his gaze on her, her focus shifted to him briefly. Then her head swung back to the agents.

Patches nudged his leg with her nose a few times and he pet her head.

"Sorry, Patches. You're right. We need to be working."

Although yesterday had been horrific, with people bleeding and crying and the gazebo blazing, the aftermath of the destruction was terrible, too. The once-cheerful white gazebo was now a pile of charred wood, splintered edges reaching into the air. The ground beside it was burned and bloodied. Scattered across the park were discarded personal items that hadn't yet been tagged and collected as evidence. The FBI's Evidence Response Team members walked among them, gathering anything relevant.

Somehow, it all felt more jarring after the awkward bliss of his morning. While Keara had showered, he'd made scrambled eggs. They'd eaten at her kitchen table and he'd pretended not to notice when she fell for Patches's sad eyes and fed her some under the table.

He'd never dated anyone in law enforcement, despite working so closely with them, despite some mutual interest a few years ago when he'd been in DC. He'd never wanted the constant fear that came along with it. But Keara? His gaze darted to her once more, took in the serious determination in every line of her body. Being with Keara would be worth it.

The four hundred miles between Desparre and Anchorage wasn't ideal, but it suddenly didn't seem impossible.

The bigger hurdle was Keara herself. Her reaction to waking up next to him this morning had been equal parts adorable and frustrating. But even if she was willing to try and pursue something long-distance, would her heart really be in it? Or would she never be able to truly give him a chance while her past was unresolved? Her words at the police station ran through his mind:

What scares me is the idea that I'll never be able to solve Juan's murder. And that as long as it remains unsolved, I'll never be able to fully move forward myself.

As he stared at her, hoping this case would be able to shed light on her husband's murder, would be able to give her that closure, he also hoped he could find a way to breach her walls even if it didn't.

She'd been closed off for years, running away to Alaska but never able to escape her husband's unsolved murder. It probably made her feel like a failure in some ways, and it wouldn't matter how often someone told her that wasn't true. She'd always wonder if she should have done more, if she should have insisted on staying on the case. He didn't need training in psych to guess that. At the very least, he wanted her to find some peace, and maybe it could be with him.

Patches nudged him again, harder this time, and Jax smiled down at her. "I know. Let's do some work."

He angled his arm toward the big tree behind the gazebo, with fresh tape around it marking it as part of the crime scene.

She tilted her head at him, as if questioning why there were no people in the direction he was telling her to go. But she walked that way anyway, periodically glancing back to make sure he was following.

This wasn't part of his job, but he needed to see the symbol himself, needed to evaluate how similar it was to all the others he'd seen in case files yesterday.

The white spruce was charred like the gazebo, strips of wood dangling from the tree. The lower leaves were charred, too, and a few branches had snapped off. But on the side facing away from the gazebo was a familiar set of loops. It wasn't an exact match to the other symbols, but only because they all had some small variation—mostly due to the materials used. This one was neatly carved, suggesting that the person who'd done it was skilled with a knife, and Jax couldn't help but think of the way Keara's husband had been murdered. With one quick slice across the neck.

A chill darted up his arms and Jax shivered, his gaze going to the surrounding forest, dense with trees and places to hide. He didn't have a lot of experience with serial bombers, but it wouldn't surprise him to learn that they liked to stay close, admire their work.

Woof!

Patches's reminder that he needed to get to his own job—and hers—was overlaid by Anderson calling, "Jax!"

The agent was standing across the street from the park, beside a couple Jax remembered from yesterday. When he'd first seen them, they'd had a young girl between them. Now the woman had a hand curved protectively over her stomach, which had just enough of a swell to tell him the reason she'd climbed into an ambulance yesterday, despite looking okay. She'd been checking on her baby.

Jax jogged over, Patches at his heels.

He hadn't had a chance to meet the family yesterday before they'd all taken off, the dad and daughter jumping into their car and following the ambulance out of Desparre. He was surprised to see them back here today.

"Jax is our Victim Specialist and Patches here is a therapy dog," Anderson introduced them. He gestured to the petite Black woman with worried eyes. "This is Imani." Then he motioned to the man beside her, a mountain of a guy whose thick beard and pale skin patchy with anger made him look like someone who could handle Alaska's wild terrain. "And her husband, Wesley."

"Nice to meet you," Jax said. When he noticed Imani eyeing Patches, he added, "She's technically still a puppy. If you want to pet her, she'll love it."

A smile peeked free and Imani reached her hand out toward Patches, who rushed over and sat on her feet.

Wesley pet her, too, keeping his other arm wrapped protectively around his wife. "We saw you at the park yesterday," Wesley finally said.

Jax nodded, letting the couple lead the conversation, knowing that Anderson had called him over for a reason.

"You were taking to the chief after she helped the officer who was hurt." Wesley and his wife shared a glance full of worry. "Is he okay?"

"He's critical." Jax told them the news Keara had gotten this morning. "But he's a fighter."

"It's our fault," Imani said, her voice tearful.

"We called him over and that's when the blast went off."

"That's not your fault," Jax said. Deep down, she knew it. But it often helped victims to hear someone else say it. "But why did you call for him?"

Anderson nodded at him as Imani and Wesley both pet Patches faster, their anxiety suddenly palpable.

"We saw this guy skulking in the woods by the gazebo," Imani said.

Jax's pulse leaped as Anderson leaned in. Had the guy they'd seen been lurking there because he was carving a symbol into the tree behind the gazebo?

"We were here with our daughter," Wesley continued. "We were heading to the swings when we spotted him. It's a park. Why does anyone need to be hiding in the woods? Unless he's there to watch kids. So we called the officers over. We hoped they could talk to the guy or scare him off."

"Who was it?" Anderson asked. "Did you recognize this guy?"

Imani shook her head. "No. We're new to Desparre. We don't know that many people yet. After the blast, he was gone."

"What did he look like?" Anderson asked.

"He was white," Imani said. "In his thirties, probably. Brown hair, I think."

Excitement thrummed along Jax's skin and he

suddenly understood how the FBI agents probably felt when they got a promising lead. He'd seen it on their faces before, the sudden thrill of the chase, but he'd never felt it so intensely himself until now.

Rodney Brown had reddish-blond hair, but from a distance it might seem brown. And he was white, would be in his thirties now.

"Anything else you remember?" Anderson pressed. "Height, maybe? Or facial hair?"

Imani shook her head. "No facial hair. But he was pretty tall. Close to my husband's height, I think."

Jax frowned, studying Wesley, who was probably only an inch shorter than Jax's six foot one. Rodney was five foot eight. Then again, the distance between the swing set and the woods was probably twenty feet. If the guy had been skulking close to the trees, maybe that had thrown off her perception, made it hard to get a good look. Plus, a bomb had gone off shortly after she'd seen him.

Then again, maybe it hadn't been Rodney she'd seen. Maybe it was Rodney's elusive roommate.

KEARA SLIPPED INSIDE the police station. She checked in quickly with Sam, who was sitting at the front desk again today, then let out a relieved breath when she reached the empty bullpen.

She'd been at the bomb site and talking to

members of the community since 7 a.m. Checking the time on her phone confirmed it was now past 3 p.m. She hadn't stopped for lunch and there was only so long the scrambled eggs Jax had cooked that morning could hold her. She didn't have an appetite.

Not after seeing the blood staining her park. Not after talking to the hospital, hearing the words *extremely critical* and *coma* when she'd asked about both Nate and Talise. But her stomach growled and her head pounded, and the coffeepot in the bullpen was calling her name. So was a quick break and a little solitude, before heading back out to talk to more people, find out if anyone had seen something that might help them find the bomber.

After dumping the sludge at the bottom of the pot that someone had brewed early that morning, Keara started a fresh one. Then she leaned against the wall, started to close her eyes.

Just before they drifted shut, she saw the stack of files on her desk through the glass walls of her office. The cases with the symbols.

Technically, they all belonged to the FBI. She probably wasn't even supposed to look at them. She definitely wasn't supposed to have them.

Pushing herself away from the wall, Keara grabbed the coffee carafe and poured everything that had brewed so far into a mug. Then she strode into her office, pushed the door shut and sat at her desk, staring at the stack of *Yes* files she and Jax had been so excited about yesterday.

There were four murders and an arson in those files. Add in the murder of Celia Harris in Houston and the bombs in Luna and Desparre and what did it all mean?

Keara slapped her hand against the desk in frustration, making it sting. Then she took a long sip of her coffee, willing the headache away, and got to work.

First, the murders. Celia Harris had been abducted, left in an alley, her killing brutal, from multiple stab wounds. She'd been a tough victim to grab, a pillar of the community with young kids and a husband at home. The symbol had been spray-painted onto the wall behind where her body was found. That had been seven years ago in Texas.

Skipping over the arson for now, Keara opened up the next murder. Five years ago, in Nebraska. The victim was a nineteen-year-old boy, on his way home from college. He'd disappeared from one side of town, only to show up on the opposite side a day later, with the symbol drawn in permanent marker across his back. He'd been killed in the time in between, from blunt force trauma to the head. He was a popular kid, a basketball star at his college. But he'd also been brought up on two sets of sexual assault charges and was estranged from his parents.

Four years ago, in Iowa. The victim was a middle-aged man, an ex-marathon runner scheduled to speak at the small town's high school track meet. The event was a big deal in the town and when he hadn't shown up, it had caused a huge uproar. His body being found later that night in a cornfield was the biggest crime they'd seen in more than a decade. He'd been shot three times, the symbol drawn thickly in pen on his arm.

Three years ago, in South Dakota. The victim was a popular middle school teacher who'd survived a heart attack the year before. She'd been grabbed and killed within a few hours, but a witness to the kidnapping had only been able to say her killer was a white male. She was strangled, found on a playground with the symbol spray-painted on the slide behind her.

Two years ago, in Montana. The victim was the newly elected mayor of a small town, with deeply polarizing views. He'd been last seen staggering drunk out of a bar. He was found a day later, in his own backyard, dead from a blow to the head. The medical examiner hadn't been able to determine if he'd fallen and cracked his own skull open or if someone had done it for him, but there had been a strange symbol spray-painted on the back of his house.

Keara stared at the glass wall into the bullpen of the station she'd come to call her own. The symbol undeniably connected these cases in some way, but the manner of death was different across all of them, the symbol never exact. It was possible there was a single killer making his way north to Alaska, committing one murder a year. Perhaps there'd been another crime in the gap after Montana and before the two bombs in Alaska, maybe in Canada while he made his way farther north.

Maybe one person had committed the murders and someone else—someone with the same knowledge of the symbol—had set the fire and the bombs.

She flipped open the arson case from Oklahoma six years ago. A brand-new rec center, the pride of the community, had opened the week before. The fire had destroyed half of it and damaged the other half so badly that it would have needed to be razed anyway. The city had never rebuilt it. Behind the rec center, on the brand-new basketball court, the symbol had been spray-painted from one end to the other.

Frowning at the case, Keara downed the last of her coffee and debated getting more. But even though it was calming her headache, her too-empty stomach was protesting. Setting the mug aside, Keara leaned back in her chair.

How similar was setting a fire and setting off bombs? They seemed pretty different to her, both from the practical standpoint of knowing how to do it and from the potential motivations. But maybe the killer was also the arsonist and the bomber had just gotten started.

It didn't feel right. No matter how she arranged the crimes in her mind, it didn't make sense. She couldn't imagine one person killing in so many different ways, with so many different victim types. And she couldn't imagine a pair of killers grabbing victims together, then randomly switching to arson, then later to bombings.

But she wasn't a psychologist. What she needed was Jax's insight.

A brief laugh escaped. Yeah, she wanted Jax's help right now, but that wasn't the only thing she wanted from him. She wished he were sitting across from her to lend his quiet support, too. So she could stare into his dark brown eyes and calm the frustration boiling inside her over all the pieces of this case that didn't quite fit together.

It had been a long time since she'd wanted to work with a man on a case in quite this way. Seven years, to be exact.

Guilt flooded, followed by an image of Juan staring contemplatively at her. The ache of missing him had faded with time, but moving on now would be a betrayal of everything they'd had together.

She was a cop and her husband had been murdered. There couldn't be room for anything else until she'd found the person responsible and made him pay.

Chapter Fourteen

If Jax was home in Anchorage on a Friday night, he'd be having dinner with friends, or maybe talking a couple of the agents into taking him to the shooting range. He'd thought he was mostly finished with the travel when he'd left the Rapid Deployment Team. But Friday night while he was in the middle of a big investigation with a lot of victims who needed him was just another night.

Tonight, though, instead of wanting to grab a quiet dinner and crash, Jax wanted to see Keara. "What do you think, Patches?"

She seemed to know exactly what he was thinking, because her tail started to wag as she stared up at him.

The two of them were on the outskirts of Desparre, back at the diner where he'd met Keara on Monday. Knowing they'd let Patches in had made it an obvious choice for a break. He'd ordered a sandwich. Enough to calm his grumbling stomach, but not so much that he couldn't eat again if Keara was up for dinner. Beside him, Patches was happily chewing the treat the restaurant owner had handed her, ignoring the dog food Jax had brought.

"Spoiled," he told her and she wagged her tail again.

Giving her a quick pat on the head, he dialed Keara, anxious to hear her voice. Although they'd gone to the crime scene together that morning, she'd left way before he had, to canvass the community. He'd spent the day in Desparre, too, but he'd been focused on the victims and families with the biggest emotional need. He and Keara had talked to the same people several times today, but never at the same time.

He missed her.

Her phone rang and rang. Just when he was expecting voice mail to pick up, Keara answered, sounding distracted. "Hello?"

"It's Jax," he told her, although he assumed she knew it from the display on her phone since she'd long since entered his contact information.

He could hear papers shuffling in the pause that followed and then finally she sighed and asked, "Did you speak to Imani and Wesley again today? Did you see the artist's rendering of the person they saw near the woods?"

After Jax had left to talk to more victims— starting with the families of Officer Nate Dreymond and Talise Poitra—Anderson had called in a sketch artist to work with the couple. He'd asked Anderson to send him the picture once it was finished.

"Yeah," he said. "I mean, people change. The picture we have of Rodney Brown is from seven years ago. But—"

"It doesn't look like him," Keara cut him off. "The nose is wrong. The cheekbones are higher. I know Rodney could have started going bald in the past seven years, but the hair seems off, too."

"Sketches aren't perfect," Jax reminded her. "Imani and Wesley weren't that close to the guy and it sounds like he tried to get out of view when he saw them looking at him."

"I know. But the thing is, I spent the afternoon reviewing the cases your system spit out. I know we already agreed the bombings don't seem connected to the earlier crimes, but Jax, I'm not sure any of them are connected."

Jax frowned and set down his sandwich. Since the second bomb had gone off, he'd been thinking they were off base, too. But there was some reason the same symbol was showing up across so many cases. He couldn't imagine a group of killers across the country, all equally skilled at evading police and all committing one crime before going dormant. "It could be a pair," Jax reminded her. "Rodney and his roommate."

"Maybe," Keara agreed, but she didn't sound convinced. "Jax, the thing is, we flagged all of the cases based on the symbols. I even considered sending the symbol to an anthropologist in case it has some kind of ancient significance, but it doesn't seem worth it. It's too rough and random, with nothing to indicate it means anything at all. I mean, you're a trained psychologist, and you haven't seen anything in it to give us a clue to its meaning. I went back and reviewed the details of the cases, too. They're just as…inconsistent. Victimology is all over the place, and the MO is different each time, too. I've never chased down a bomber before and I've never had a serial murder case, either, but nothing I know about them fits what I saw in those case files. If you take the symbol out of it, they don't seem connected at all."

"But we can't take the symbol out of it," Jax reminded her.

She let out a frustrated laugh. "No kidding. But the victims don't fit. Jax, we've got a rec center that was empty and set on fire. The murder victims were a female baker in her thirties who was a pillar of the community, a nineteen-year-old college boy with a couple of sexual assault charges on his record, a fiftyish man who used to run marathons, a popular middle school teacher in her forties and a sixtyish man with a really polarizing platform who was just elected as mayor. Then we've got the bombings, where we haven't identified the target. What ties all of these people together?"

Leaning back against the vinyl seat, Jax contemplated the list Keara had just given him. She was right. They didn't make sense as targets of the same person. They didn't even make sense as targets of two people.

The explosions in Luna and Desparre weren't the first bombings he'd assisted on. And he'd worked with two victims of a serial killer that the FBI had managed to rescue, helping them through the legal process for almost a year. He wasn't a profiler, but he'd learned way more about how serial killers worked during that case than he'd ever wanted to know.

Most serial killers had a specific type. Even when there wasn't specifically a sexual component to the crime itself, many of them were sexually motivated. Such a wide range of victims wasn't unheard of, but it was unusual. And when it happened, there was almost always a specific method of killing that was most important to the killer.

Still, the symbol… It felt almost like a signature to him, a specific thing the killer felt compelled to do, something that marked the crime as theirs. They might be able to change their MO, but a signature would remain.

But was drawing a series of loops on or near the bodies really a compulsive behavior? Or was it being used by a group of criminals, maybe individuals who'd found each other somehow and made a pact to leave behind the symbols to confuse authorities?

Except if that was the case, then why hadn't they seen additional matching crimes in each jurisdiction?

Rubbing his head, Jax admitted, "It doesn't make sense to me. I talked to Ben a bit about it today. He had a quick look at the cases we pulled. He admitted that if we'd found a series of bombs with the symbol, they'd be chasing that lead full-throttle. But across singular killings like this, he thinks it's far less likely to be connected."

"The FBI is still looking into it?" Keara pressed.

"Yeah. But obviously, the bombs are the first priority. Two so close together are a pattern that can't be ignored. And then there's the psychology of a bomber versus a killer."

"Bombers like chaos," Keara said. "They like to create fear and destruction."

"Yeah," Jax agreed. "And a serial killer who murders his victims up close probably isn't going to want to watch from a distance, like with arson or a bomb. It seems like two different personality types to me."

"And unless our murderer is also just determined to try out every method of killing possible, the single murders in each state don't really seem connected, either," Keara said.

Jax sighed. He'd initiated the call feeling hopeful, almost nervous. He'd been planning to suggest they get dinner and distract themselves from the stress and horror of the case. He'd been hoping dinner might lead to an offer for him and Patches to stay on her couch again, even though he'd confirmed that the Royal Desparre allowed dogs. He didn't expect her to join him on the couch this time, but right now being close to her was enough.

Now he felt exhausted and discouraged. Even Patches, catching his mood, let out a whine and lay on the ground.

"Where do we go from here?" Keara prompted when he didn't speak for a minute.

Jax rubbed his head, pushing aside his sandwich, no longer hungry. "I have no idea." And that was true of more than just the case. Equally frustrating was his inability to help her personally, help her move forward. Without that, there was no chance of this attraction between them going anywhere.

KEARA HADN'T BEEN back to Texas in over a year. Even then, so many years after her husband's murder, being in Houston had given her anxiety, brought back all of her anger and frustration over Juan's case having gone cold. But maybe it was time to return. The thoughts ran through her mind the next morning as she lay in bed.

Once the bombing was solved, she could take some personal time. If she could convince the Houston PD to reopen the case, if she could work it unofficially, maybe she could finally get some closure.

Seven years was long enough. She needed to

be able to move forward. And for the first time, she wanted to truly move forward, to start living her life fully again.

It wasn't hard to identify the reason. She'd never known a man like Jax Diallo, never connected so quickly to anyone.

He lived on the other side of the state, but that might actually be a good thing. It would keep any relationship from moving too quickly, from getting too serious before she was ready. Because wanting to move forward wasn't the same as wanting to dive headfirst into a serious relationship. Still, she didn't want to say goodbye when the bombings were solved.

She was pretty sure he was interested. Best of all, although he worked for the FBI, he wasn't a law-enforcement officer. He wasn't constantly running into danger. He was helping victims, but he wasn't interacting with the suspects.

Sure, there were no guarantees. Everyone faced some level of risk just walking around in the world. Being a cop for so many years had definitely taught her that. But Jax was a much safer man to love than Juan had ever been.

The unexpected thought made anxiety and guilt bubble up and Keara shoved off her covers, stepped onto the cold wood floor in her bedroom. *Love.* That was an emotion way off in the future, if ever. Right now she had much bigger things to worry about.

Glancing at the clock on her bedside table, Keara groaned. Almost 8 a.m. It might have been Saturday, but she still had a long day ahead of her and she had planned to get an early start.

So much for that plan. Debating whether to jump into a fast shower or just start making phone calls, Keara opted for the phone. She started with the hospital, heart pounding faster as she waited for news on Nate and Talise.

"Both of their conditions are the same," the nurse who finally came on the line told her.

She tried to quell the disappointment. At least they weren't deteriorating. Both had faced serious injuries. Talise had gone through emergency surgery for her leg and Nate had gotten his head stitched up, only for doctors to open it up again a few hours later to release intracranial pressure.

Hanging up with the hospital, Keara sighed and headed to the kitchen. She couldn't stop herself from glancing at the couch where she'd slept—much less fitfully—the night before last. Couldn't stop herself from wishing Jax and Patches were sitting there to greet her again this morning.

When she'd spoken to Jax late last night, he'd been at a diner on the outskirts of Desparre. They'd talked about the case and then he'd had to let her go, to take a call from one of the agents. Even though she'd gone through everything she'd needed to tell him about the cases, she'd half expected him to call back. When she hadn't heard from him, she'd heated up a frozen dinner, done a little kickboxing to combat her frustration, then headed to bed.

As she turned on her coffeepot, Keara pulled up Jax's number. Before she could hit Call, her phone rang. It was a number she didn't recognize.

"Chief Hernandez," she answered.

"This is Ben Nez."

The last of Keara's sleepiness cleared away. Was there a break in the case? "Agent Nez. What's happening?"

"We've been running down all of the victims in the two bombings, trying to nail down a potential target."

From the beginning, she'd heard the FBI theorizing that a specific target was likely, since the bombs could have easily been placed in more populated areas or spots that would have gotten more publicity. Although the bombs had definitely made the news in and around Desparre and Luna, they hadn't been large or spectacular enough to make much of a blip on the national news.

"Any luck?" she asked when he paused.

"Well, I wanted your take on something. We just discovered that one of the people who was killed at the Luna bombing is actually related to a victim in Desparre."

"Who is it?" Keara asked, frowning. The connection was news to her.

"Aiden DeMarco was the victim in Luna. He

posted the idea about the soccer game on the chat room, so the bomber would have definitely known he'd be there. He was eighteen, planned to leave Alaska to go to college in California. We looked into him early on, didn't see any reason for him to be targeted, but we could have missed something. His aunt on his mom's side, Gina Metner, was injured in Desparre."

"I know Gina," Keara said. The woman was a transplant from the lower forty-eight. She'd moved up to Alaska to be near her sister and escape from a violent ex. But the ex had since died and Gina had decided she wanted even more solitude than Luna offered, so she'd found herself a home in Desparre. She worked part-time at the library in Luna and part-time at the grocery store with Talise.

"Gina talked about her sister and her nephew, but I didn't know his name," Keara told Ben. "I didn't realize he'd been killed in the bombing."

"Can you think of anyone with a grudge against Gina?"

"No one living." Keara explained about the violent ex, then added, "Gina and I got to talking a year ago, when she first decided to move to Desparre. She gave me a bit of a rundown on her life. But otherwise, she's pretty quiet. She's got a couple of friends here we can talk to, but I can't imagine her having made a ton of enemies since she moved to Alaska two years ago."

"We spoke to Gina already," Ben said. "She said the same thing. It could be a coincidence." He sighed. "But I was hoping we might have stumbled across the connection we've been trying to find."

"Gina wasn't badly hurt in the bombing," Keara said. "She was leaving the park when the bomb went off. She got checked out since the blast initially impacted her hearing, but she got the all clear to go home the same day. The only thing she needed was a couple of stitches and not even directly from the blast. It was when the explosion knocked her down and she hit the pavement."

"Right. So if the bomber was targeting her and he was nearby, maybe the couple who spotted him and called the police over threw him off. Maybe he was distracted and ducked into the woods to hide, didn't get farther away quickly enough. He wouldn't have wanted to be that close when the bomb went off. Assuming the bomber is the same person Imani and Wesley saw near the tree with the carving on it," Ben added.

"Luna and Desparre are pretty small towns. It's not really surprising that two of the victims would be related."

"Yeah, well, you know what they say about all the bases," Ben said.

Keara mumbled an agreement, trying not to let him hear how disheartened she felt. This kind of investigation was more like a marathon than a sprint. A bomber savvy enough to have set off the bomb in Luna—which hadn't yielded any significant leads more than a week later—probably wasn't going to be easy to find.

"What about the sketch of the suspect?" Keara asked.

She hadn't recognized him. Neither had anyone on her force. That was a little bit surprising if he lived around here, since they were a small town. Then again, Desparre was known for being the sort of place where you could come to disappear. They had a lot of land to get lost in and if you wanted to stay off everyone's radar, there was a whole mountain to hide on. If the bomber was hiding here, it wouldn't be the first time the town had a criminal in their midst.

"We're still showing the sketch around," Ben told her. "So far no one knows this guy."

If the bomber *was* the same person who'd been responsible for the murders and arson in the lower forty-eight, it made sense that no one knew him. He'd be staying far below the radar. But there had been five days between the Luna bombing and the one in her park. It had now been two days since the blast that had been close enough to shake the walls of the Desparre police station.

If he'd gone from a once-a-year, once-a-location killer to a serial bomber, how much time did they have before he struck again?

Chapter Fifteen

When Keara walked into the police station half an hour later, the rest of her department, and most of the FBI agents, were already there. Thankfully, it looked like they were just getting started.

She nodded at her officers, who were all working serious overtime. Since they were a small town, they were constantly on call. But the station was typically closed from 9 p.m. until 9 a.m. In the past two days most of them had been there until midnight.

Then her gaze was drawn to Jax. As soon as she made eye contact, he smiled at her. Patches did him one better, letting out a happy *woof!* and racing across the room, sliding to a slightly uncoordinated stop at her feet.

Keara laughed, grateful for the moment of levity. She wondered if the intelligent therapy dog had done it on purpose. "Hi, Patches."

Patches wagged her tail, staring up expectantly until Keara pet her.

Then Jax was standing beside her, his presence somehow managing to make her more calm and nervous at the same time.

"Today we're hoping to get more information on motive and our potential suspect," Ben announced, his voice carrying over the few conversations and making everyone go quiet.

"Since you know the residents here better than we do, we're hoping to pair agents and officers," Ben said. "The goal is twofold. First, to figure out if anyone knows of a reason one of the victims might have been targeted or anyone who'd want to do them harm. Second, to show them the sketch we got from two of the people on the scene. See if anyone recognizes him."

"What about me and Patches?" Jax piped up.

"We're hoping you can drive back to Luna, talk to Aiden DeMarco's family and see if they have any idea why both their son and his aunt might have been targeted."

Jax nodded, looking unsurprised, and Keara hid her disappointment.

He wasn't an agent. He wouldn't have been paired with her anyway. And if he had been, she would have needed to protest. Although talking to residents wasn't dangerous in theory, it could lead them to a bomber. Hell, they could actually end up knocking on the door of the bomber. Keara didn't know everyone who lived here, especially those who chose to hide on the mountain, who didn't want to be known.

Desparre was a small town only in terms of population. When it came to size—and the distance backup had to travel if you needed them—it was definitely large.

"I've got a list of pairings," Ben continued, "and a stack of printed sketches you can show people. That way, anyone with low vision won't have to squint at your phones. And there's no chance of anyone trying to snatch that phone away from you."

He said the last part like he'd experienced it and Keara raised her eyebrows at Jax, who just shrugged in response.

"Does that work for you, Chief Hernandez?" Ben called across the room.

Everyone's attention swiveled her way and she nodded, appreciating that he wasn't just trying to railroad over her small department. The FBI had more experience, but her officers knew the area and the people better. "The plan makes sense. Everyone stay safe out there. If you get a lead, call it in on the radio before you pursue it. And make sure you stay in contact. I want everyone checking in with regular status updates."

Her officers nodded somberly. Normally, she might have gotten a couple of rolled eyes at that request, but not today.

Policing a small town could get tedious, make you let down your guard. You thought you knew the people, thought you knew the dangers. But out here, where it was common to take calls alone, communication was their best defense. It was something she preached on a regular basis.

"I've got pairings up here," Ben announced, and everyone headed his way.

Keara turned to Jax and lowered her voice. "Did you talk to Ben and Anderson any more about the other cases and the inconsistencies?"

"Yeah. They're as confused as we are. They think our best chance of figuring out what the symbol means is to follow the other leads right now." Jax's lips pursed. "I still think there has to be a way to use the symbol to find the killer, but I don't know how."

It wasn't his job to know how. His psychological insight was useful, but he'd already stepped into profiler territory by confirming that the symbol was important, that it linked these crimes somehow. Jax wasn't an agent or a detective. It was her job—and Ben's and Anderson's and all of the other agents and officers—to follow the leads and uncover the bomber.

"You should focus on the victims," she told him. "I've seen the difference you and Patches make."

Woof!

Keara smiled and pet Patches more, as Jax stared at her pensively, his expression unreadable.

Had he felt insulted that she didn't think he should run leads? Would he feel the same way if he knew it made her more comfortable pursuing something romantic with him when he was sticking safely on the outskirts of the case?

His lips twitched, like he could read her thoughts.

"Let's get going," Ben said and Keara gave Patches one more pet, nodded goodbye to Jax and hurried over to see who she'd be running leads with today.

"It's you and me," Anderson announced before she reached the more senior agent.

"Great," Keara said. Anderson seemed pretty easygoing and professional. "Where are we headed?"

"Up the mountain. The place most likely for a bomber to be holed up, don't you think?"

"Let's do it," she agreed. She glanced back once more at Jax as she headed out the door and she could have sworn she saw him mouth the words, *Be careful.*

As she led Anderson over to her police SUV— specially equipped to handle Desparre's rough roads and dangerous weather—she wondered if Jax worried about her. She wanted him far away from danger, didn't want to have to fear finding another man she cared for the way she'd found Juan. But she'd understood the dangers with Juan because she faced them herself. What must it be like for Jax, somewhat on the outside, to hear that she was heading into a remote area that would be a good place for a bomber to hide?

Pulling out her phone before she hopped into the car, she sent Jax a quick text:

Let me know how it goes with the victims today.
I'll keep you updated, too.

It felt like the sort of thing she'd text if she
was actually dating him. Hoping she wasn't making assumptions about plans that weren't recipro-
cated, she tucked her phone back into her pocket.

Climbing into the driver's seat, she asked Anderson, "Which part of the mountain? You know
it's pretty massive, right?"

"We have one of your veterans paired up with
one of our longtime agents. They're hitting the
far side of the mountain. I thought we'd handle
the closer side. We'll do as much as we can today
and see what pops."

"Sounds good," Keara agreed as she started
up her vehicle.

Some people headed this far north in Alaska
just to find a good adventure. But most of the
people who landed in Desparre were looking to
be left alone. Usually, there was nothing sinister
about it. Maybe they were running from a tragedy, like she was. Or maybe they were running
from a threat, like Tate Emory was. Sometimes,
though, they were hiding because the law was
after them or because the vast spaces of Alaska
seemed like a great place to stay off law-enforcement radar or hide a victim.

For the first ten minutes of their ride, Anderson
was quiet, just texting or watching out the win-

dow. Then he slid his phone into his pocket and shifted toward her. "So this symbol…"

She glanced briefly at him, then back at the road. In the spring driving up the mountain wasn't dangerous like it could be in the winter, with the heavy snow and avalanches. But the roads were still narrow, the vehicles here usually large. On a couple of occasions, she'd had to hit the brakes for an animal. Once, it had been a bear.

"What about it?" she asked. "You have a theory?"

"Maybe. I've been thinking through what Jax told me this morning about how different the victimology and MOs in each of the cases has been, even the way the symbol was written. In marker or spray paint or even pen."

"And?" Keara prompted, her hands tensing around the wheel, hoping he had a new idea that would make sense of it all.

"We know savvy criminals learn from each other. What if we've got a group of them on a dark web site, not just trading insight into how to avoid getting caught, but also sharing this symbol?"

"Why?" Keara asked. "You think it's a way to mark their own kills? Keep track and try to outdo each other? But wouldn't using the same symbol defeat the purpose?"

"No," Anderson replied. "I was thinking more like a game, coordinating a single symbol across all these different places and crimes to confuse police."

The tension across the back of Keara's shoulders and neck notched tighter. "That makes sense," she admitted. Not only would it confuse the authorities if they connected the crimes through the symbols, but it also added a cooperative-competitive element that she could imagine appealing to a killer or a bomber. Attention from an eager audience without the risk, since they were all criminals, too.

If Anderson was right, the bomber wasn't committing the other crimes. If the communication was happening in a chat room on a dark web site, then the bomber probably didn't even know who the other people were.

A familiar frustration welled up. Even if they caught the bomber, would it get them any closer to Juan's killer?

Or was her dream of finally solving his cold case just that?

Chapter Sixteen

Talking to Aiden DeMarco's parents had been brutal. All of their dreams for their eldest son had been shattered in a single moment. Jax and Patches had been able to offer them support over the whole day that Jax knew they needed. And he'd managed to gather as much information as he could about what Aiden's parents—who'd been nearby when the bomb went off—had seen. But they had no idea why anyone would target their son or his aunt. Neither did Jax.

Frankly, he didn't think anyone *had* targeted either one.

Halfway through the day Ben had called him after checking in with Anderson. He'd shared the other agent's theory about a group of criminals coordinating on a dark web site. It had Ben excited and the cybercrime unit back in Anchorage pivoting to the theory as a priority.

If they were right, a serial bomber with the knowledge and connections to access a site like that probably wasn't using bombs as a messy way to kill a few specific people. He was way more likely to be an indiscriminate killer more interested in watching the chaos he created.

The fact that they hadn't found other bomb sites with the symbol could have meant his earlier bombs weren't as perfected and the symbol he'd intended to leave behind had been destroyed in the blast. Or evidence had been poorly collected or missed. Either way, this seemed like a practiced criminal.

Someone like that was prepared. He was well hidden, might have even booby-trapped his home in case law enforcement ever figured out his location.

Keara was driving around on top of a secluded mountain, searching for him.

The idea had lodged a ball of fear in his chest that had just gotten worse as the day turned into evening and the sun set, descending the town into darkness.

He'd heard from her again early in the afternoon, letting him know they were at the top of the mountain and hadn't had luck so far, but nothing since then. Jax had resisted calling or texting her, not wanting to distract her at a crucial moment. She was a seasoned law-enforcement officer with more than a decade of experience under her belt, about half of it in a busy city with a much higher crime rate.

Right now, though, making the lengthy drive back from Luna with Patches asleep in the backseat, he'd been alone with his worry for too long. He'd be at the Desparre police station in five minutes, but he wasn't sure if anyone would be there since it was after nine. He knew Ben had gone back to the hotel, but he didn't know whether Anderson and Keara had made it down the mountain yet.

Was this what it would be like if he could talk her into giving a relationship with him a chance? This constant fear about whether she'd make it home? Was that something he'd be able to handle long-term? Because despite the distance between Anchorage and Desparre, if he and Keara started something, he couldn't imagine ever wanting to stop.

"Call Keara," he told his phone.

From the backseat, Patches let out a quiet *woof*, then he heard her sitting up.

It rang twice before Keara picked up. "Hi, Jax."

She sounded happy to hear from him, but he could tell from the exhaustion underneath that the trip hadn't yielded anything promising.

Woof! Patches chimed in loudly.

Keara laughed. "Hi, Patches."

"I take it no one recognized the picture?" Jax asked.

"We had a couple of vague 'he looks sort of familiar, but I don't know where from' kind of answers. But no one had a name and address handy."

"So he might live up on that mountain," Jax said, feeling more encouraged than Keara sounded.

"He might," Keara agreed. "We'll definitely

have officers canvassing again tomorrow. The thing is, the mountain is huge. People stake out land and build without permits or actual ownership. It's not like we can stop them if we don't know they're up there. Some of it is pretty far off the beaten path. And if you've got someone willing to venture off the road a ways—which we definitely do—it can be nearly impossible to find them."

"It sounds like the stereotype of Alaska," Jax commented. "That you can just venture off and get yourself completely off the grid, if you're not afraid of the harsh elements."

He'd seen some truth to that when he'd gotten here, but Anchorage was a pretty developed, populated area. Still, he could drive about an hour outside town and find solitude at a glacier if he wanted. He and Patches had done it a half dozen times since moving here and only once had he run into another person.

Compared to Anchorage, Desparre was the wild north.

"Well, sometimes the best thing about a place can also be the worst," Keara said.

He heard her turn signal in the background and the knot in his chest loosened up, knowing she had to be off the mountain to need a turn signal. "Are you going back to the station now?"

"I've already been there. I dropped Anderson

off and now I'm almost home. I was just about to call you, actually."

"Oh, yeah?" His long day suddenly seemed less exhausting.

"How did the trip to Luna go?"

"Nothing new, really." He sighed, remembering the devastation on the parents' faces, the confusion and grief in every movement of his three younger siblings.

"I guess I'm not surprised." He heard her car door slam, then her voice got more distant, maybe as she juggled the phone and opened the door to her house.

"Me, either, but I was hopeful. The fact that one of the Luna casualties, Aiden DeMarco, was the one who set up the soccer game and then his aunt was also hurt in a bomb? It seemed like maybe there was something to that."

"I don't think this bomber was after a specific—" She broke off on a mumbled curse.

"Keara?"

"Someone's been in my house."

"What?"

"My office doesn't look right."

"What do you mean? Are you sure?"

From the backseat, Patches whined, picking up on his anxiety.

"Yeah, I'm sure."

Her voice was hard and determined and he imagined her pulling her gun from its holster.

Jax punched down on the gas, wishing he was closer to her house. "I'm coming to you. Get out of the house, Keara."

"I'm a police chief, Jax. And I'm already inside. I can handle a walk-through."

"You need backup!"

"I'll call them," she promised, "But I need to go."

"No! Just wait for backup. That has to be proced—"

"*Jax.* It doesn't look like anyone is in here." Her voice had dropped to a whisper and he had to strain to hear her final, "I'll call you when it's all clear."

"No—"

He swore as he realized she'd hung up, then hit the gas harder, taking curves too fast. If a Desparre police officer pulled him over, all the better. Then he'd have backup.

He wasn't an agent. He'd gone to the shooting range with the Anchorage agents enough to be a pretty good shot, but he didn't carry a weapon. That wasn't how Victim Specialists worked. On some level probably the agents' teasing about him being an "agent wannabe" bothered him because it was true. Some part of him would have loved to get into the nitty gritty of an investigation, follow a trail of clues until an arrest and been the one to slap handcuffs on perpetrators. But he'd never pursued it, knowing the role he had now would ultimately fulfill him more.

At this moment, though, he wished he'd made a different decision. Wished he could be real help to Keara.

"Call Desparre PD," he told his phone as Patches whimpered.

"Desparre Police Department," a tired voice answered. It was familiar, but he wasn't sure which officer had phone duty that night.

"It's Jax Diallo," he blurted. "Someone broke into the chief's house. She needs backup right now."

"What?" The officer's surprise was overridden only by his sudden state of alert. "Okay, we're on it. Do you know details? Is the person still there? Are they armed?"

"I don't know. But *Keara* is there." He couldn't remember ever feeling this helpless.

"I'm sending help now," the officer told him, then hung up.

Jax punched down a bit more on the gas, even though he knew he was approaching dangerous speeds. Then he called Ben.

From the sound of the agent's voice when he answered, Jax had woken him up.

"I need agents at Keara's house. Someone broke in," Jax cut off his greeting.

He didn't bother ending the call as he whipped his vehicle into Keara's drive and slammed it into Park.

From the backseat, Patches slid across the seat and yelped.

"Sorry, Patches," he said, then added, "Stay!" as he jumped out of the SUV and closed the door behind him.

He could hear police sirens in the distance, getting closer, but the house in front of him was mostly dark, only a porch light giving him any real visibility.

It wasn't enough. For a house far from neighbors, set in the woods, it wasn't nearly enough to see if a threat lurked nearby.

Jax glanced back, watching for the police cars. But they weren't close enough yet.

He couldn't wait. He ran around to the back of his vehicle and dug underneath the spare tire, hoping the rental company wanted their renters to be prepared. Relief filled him as he found a big metal hexagon wrench. It wasn't a gun, but it was better than nothing.

He was racing toward the house, holding the wrench too tightly, when Keara stepped out the front door.

"It's empty," she told him, holstering her gun. "Whoever was in here was gone before I got home." The hard fury on her face was only undermined by the vulnerability in her eyes.

His grip on the wrench loosened and he realized his hand hurt from how tightly he'd been gripping it.

Her gaze drifted to the wrench then back up to his face. "You were going to rush in here with nothing but that?" Her lips pursed with what looked like anger, but her forehead crinkled with confusion or concern and she went silent.

He didn't bother to answer, just tried to breathe deeply, encourage his frenzied heartbeat to slow.

From the car, Patches called *Woof! Woof! Woof!*

Keara walked over to Jax, put her hand on his arm and he looped his free arm around her, yanking her against his chest.

Even with the sirens getting louder and louder, there was no way she'd miss his rapid heartbeat; no way she'd misunderstand his fear. But he didn't say anything. Right now as much as he wanted to pursue something more, they were only colleagues. He'd known her for eight days. He had no right to tell her how to manage a crime scene at her own home.

But she whispered against his chest, "I'm sorry I worried you. I should have gone outside and waited for backup."

As if her words had summoned them, a pair of trucks came screeching into her drive, portable sirens blaring.

Jax glanced behind him, letting go of Keara as officers jumped out of their vehicles, weapons ready.

Keara held up a hand. "It's all clear. But someone was in my house."

The officers holstered their weapons as Keara continued, "I don't think anything was taken. It barely looks disturbed. I think whoever was here hoped I wouldn't even realize it. But they definitely went through my office, especially all of my documents."

"Any sign of forced entry?" Charlie Quinn asked. There was exhaustion in the dark circles under his eyes and an invisible weight that seemed to pull his whole face downward, but his voice was focused and clear.

"No." Keara looked troubled as she admitted, "I'm not sure how they got in."

More vehicles raced into the drive and then FBI agents poured out.

Keara looked embarrassed as she said, "I've already cleared the house. It was a break-in, but nothing was taken."

Ben strode toward them, looking purposeful and focused. "You get a lot of break-ins around here?"

She shrugged. "Some."

"Do people know this is the police chief's home?"

She nodded slowly. "I don't advertise it, but this is a small town. So yeah, I'm sure some people have figured it out."

"Ever had any problems here before?"

She shook her head.

Ben nodded briefly at Jax, then asked Keara, "Any chance this is connected to the bombings?"

Jax's calming heartbeat took off again as he stared at Keara, watched her consider it.

"I don't know. But someone was interested in what I had in my office. I don't bring police cases home, except on a laptop, which is in my SUV. My paper files are mostly personal."

Ben nodded. "Just in case this is connected, how do you feel about letting the FBI's evidence techs go through your office?"

Keara nodded slowly. "All of our officers are trained in evidence collection. But in the interest of collaboration, that would be appreciated."

Ben nodded at her, then started calling out orders to the other agents as Keara directed her officers to head home.

Then she turned to Jax, all the vulnerability he'd seen in her eyes earlier gone now and replaced by anger. "What do you think? Why would the bomber come here? He assumed I'd have case files in my home and it would be an easier target than a downtown police station? You think he hoped to find out what we knew about him?"

Jax stared back at her, all his worry over her home being targeted fading into the background as he remembered the first time he'd seen her at the bomb site. Then the expression on her face when she'd identified that symbol for them. A symbol that, as far as they could find, hadn't appeared on a crime scene in Alaska until the Luna bombing.

"I think we were right from the beginning," he realized. "I think the bomber *is* connected to your husband's murder."

"What? *Why?*"

"I think all of the cases are connected," Jax said, the theory gaining strength in his mind as he said it out loud. "I think we just found the missing motivation."

"What do you mean?" Keara asked.

"I think the missing motivation is *you*."

Chapter Seventeen

Dread mingled with fury and residual adrenaline as Keara stared at Jax. The excitement in his gaze told her that he thought his new theory was right.

"How could I be the motivation for these bombings?" Keara asked. "I didn't have a close relationship with any of the victims—unless you count the fact that Nate works for me. I wasn't even there when the Luna bomb went off. And if he wanted to target me in Desparre, he could have come out here earlier, planted the bomb at my house."

The thought that the bomber knew where she lived, that he could have been in her house, looking through her personal items, made her home somehow feel less *hers*. The idea that he might have seen her photo album from her wedding sitting on her coffee table, might have flipped idly through the pages, smiled at the memory of killing her husband, made her fists clench.

The bomber coming here to find out if they were onto him made sense. But him setting bombs *because* of her didn't.

When Jax stayed silent, his lips twisted and his pupils rolled slightly upward, like he was still working it out in his mind, she prompted, "You need to explain this theory to me."

Behind her, the other agents had gone quiet, but stepped closer. They were all listening, too, waiting with enough patience that Keara knew they valued Jax's psychological insight as much as she did.

"What if we've stumbled on to a serial killer who isn't interested in a certain victim type or a particular weapon?" Jax asked slowly.

Keara held in her immediate rebuttal: they'd already decided this wasn't a serial killer/bomber *because* there wasn't a common victimology or MO. "Then what's his motivation?"

"He gets off on outwitting police," Jax said, a mix of surprise and certainty in his voice.

"Police in general?" Keara pressed. "So not me specifically?" She didn't like the idea either way, but the thought that a serial killer was somehow focused on her, motivated to kill because of her, was really unsettling.

"Yes," Jax said, his hand reaching out like he was going to take hers, then dropping back to his side. "Sorry. I didn't mean that it was you personally motivating him. I think he's motivated by whoever is working to solve the crime he committed. It's like a game to him—can he keep committing crimes without the police finding him?"

Keara frowned. Behind her, she could hear the agents shifting, like they were impatient and unconvinced, too.

"Every serial killer wants to outwit police," Ben spoke up. "I don't think that's enough of a motivation alone."

"Why not?" Jax countered, crossing his arms over his chest. "You thought a group of criminals were playing games by using the same symbol and laughing at police on a dark web chat room."

"Sure," Anderson said. "But—"

"Hear me out," Jax interrupted. "It could explain why there have been so many different locations. Because he's looking for a new challenge each time, a new police office to test, to see if he can find a worthy opponent."

"Or he's just trying to outrun the investigations by changing jurisdictions," Ben countered. "A lot of serial killers try that."

"Sure," Jax agreed, not looking deterred. "But you didn't think it was a serial criminal responsible for everything, because of all the differences. What about the similarities? How likely is it really that we have six different criminals—murderers, an arsonist and a bomber—all using the same symbol *and* all equally skilled at leaving behind such clean crime scenes? Not to mention, all of them only committing one—or maybe two—crimes before stopping?"

The agents behind her were silent as Jax stared at them with raised eyebrows. Keara thought about each of the case files she'd read, about the total lack of progress in each of those cases.

They'd all eventually gone cold, just like her husband's murder.

"Okay," Ben said, sounding like he was reluctantly getting on board with Jax's theory. "Then why bombs now after a series of murders and one arson?"

"Because the weapon isn't the point," Jax said, the excitement in his voice growing.

It set off an excitement in her, too, a hope that they were getting closer to finding the person responsible for all of the crimes. Including Juan's murder.

"When serial killers get away with it, they get bolder, right?" Jax asked, his gaze on Ben.

Keara shifted, so she could see them both.

On Ben's face was interest, the thrill of being on a solid lead that she recognized. The excitement was catching. All the other agents were slowly nodding.

"Usually," Ben agreed.

"Sometimes, they go for bigger challenges, too, right?" Jax leaned in and his familiar cinnamon scent wafted toward her. "They'll try to grab victims who are more high risk for them. They'll spend more time with the victims, leave the body in a more public place, maybe."

"So you think this is just a progression?" Keara asked. "He started with murders, tried an arson— and presumably got more attention with the murders, so returned to them? Then he came here and decided bombs would have a bigger impact, get more of a law-enforcement response?"

Jax nodded. "Yes. And maybe some of this was also him learning what he liked. Maybe initially he figured he'd get more of a thrill from the killing than he did. When he discovered it was actually watching the law-enforcement response—seeing the police scramble to try and find *him*—that became more of his focus."

It made sense in a weird way. Celia Harris's murder almost certainly wasn't the guy's first kill. It was too perfect, too precise, the victim too high risk, the body dumped in a place too close to public areas. He'd probably started with easier victims, people who were less likely to be missed, dumping the bodies in places he hoped they wouldn't be found. The symbol could have evolved over time, too.

"So if this is all a progression, if it's really about this guy trying to outwit the police, then what about Juan?" Keara asked as fury and grief and determination entwined inside her. "He got too close to the truth, didn't he? This guy thought he was outwitting police and then Juan showed up at his door and the bomber decided he needed to kill him, didn't he?"

Jax nodded slowly, her own pain reflected in his eyes. "That's my guess. I think you were onto something all along with Rodney—or, more likely, given that the sketch we have doesn't match Rodney, his roommate. I think Juan was killed because he got too close to the truth."

"And the crimes were much bigger than he'd ever realized," Keara finished.

KEARA'S GAZE WAS troubled as she demanded, "Do you think the bomber came here because he knew I worked here? Because he knows I'm Juan's widow?"

The agents behind her all cringed. It was barely perceptible, because they were all trained and practiced at hiding emotion. But no doubt they'd all dealt with loved ones who were afraid of one day getting the dreaded call.

Jax's heart gave a pained kick, but he tried to consider all the angles before he answered. This wasn't his job. This wasn't his specialty. Yes, he had a lot of training in psychology, a lot of experience working with the victims this type of criminal left behind. But there were other professionals out there, profilers who focused on the other side of it: knowing the mind of the criminal.

"I doubt it," he said finally. "But it can't hurt to get a profiler's thoughts on that." He glanced at Ben, who nodded slowly, but didn't seem anxious to get a second opinion.

"If I'm right, then it took him a long time to get to Alaska. If he came here for you, then why stop in so many states along the way? Why take so many years to get here? It seems like it was probably a coincidence."

"He was jumping from one jurisdiction to the next," Anderson said, "changing locations once each case went cold. Unless we just missed some of his crimes, this guy is patient."

Ben nodded. "A year is a long time in between crimes for a serial criminal, if that's really what we've got here."

"Right," Anderson said, sounding excited by Jax's new take on the perpetrator. "But for big investigations like the ones we're talking about, it seems reasonable that police would be actively investigating for a year. Those investigations would slowly ramp down until they were deemed cold and set on the back burner."

"This guy probably wouldn't know exactly when that happened," Ben said. "But once he couldn't see police activity, once the news coverage died down, he moved to a new state, studied a new victim, planned a new crime." He gave Jax an impressed look. "It makes sense. And it explains a lot of things that just wouldn't fit together otherwise. I think you're onto something here, Jax."

It would take a methodical, patient killer. But each of the cases Jax had reviewed with Keara suggested that kind of criminal. Someone who had studied how to avoid leaving forensics behind, who had watched his intended victim beforehand to avoid witnesses, who had scoped out the location he planned to leave the body. Someone who followed the police investigation, followed the officers investigating, without being noticed.

Jax flashed back to the moment he'd been driving to meet Keara and had thought someone was following him. A dark blue truck that had turned another way when Jax started driving erratically. Had it been the bomber, looking for insight on the case? Had he followed Jax in the past, maybe even to Keara's home? Had that been how he knew where she lived?

Guilt flooded, along with a rush of relief that Keara was okay. What if the bomber had been waiting in her house instead of just going through her files? What if he'd been standing in the dark with a knife, ready to do to Keara what he'd done to her husband?

The idea made nausea flood through him and he tried to push it back, tried to keep thinking through his new theory as impartially as he could.

Keara stared back at him, her eyes narrowing as if she could read his emotions.

She probably could. She was a trained investigator, after all. Would it scare her off, the intensity of his feelings for her? How had they gotten so strong, so fast?

"If this guy is following the investigation as closely as you're suggesting, and it is someone who's been here less than two years, then he's been at the scenes," Keara said with certainty. "He's been talking to people. That means someone has seen him. We need to keep circulating that sketch. Has it been shown to all of the victims and anyone else who was near the scenes at the time of the bombings?"

"We've shown it to all of the victims who are able to look at it right now," Anderson said, reminding Jax that there were still two Desparre victims in comas, still three from the Luna bomb who were critical and unresponsive, as well.

"And? No one recognized him?" Keara pressed.

"Some of them said the sketch looked kind of familiar," Ben replied. "But no one could give us a name. Same result as the general canvassing today."

"He's good at blending in," Jax said. "He's got a lot of practice fading into the background."

"This is a small town," Keara said, frustration in her voice. "We notice outsiders. Yeah, we let them have their privacy, but unless they're hiding out on the mountain all day, we see them." She frowned, a ripple of anger rushing over her features. "Of course, I thought that five years ago, too, and we had a kidnapper living among us. People knew him vaguely, but no one seemed to know who he was."

"We'll find this guy," Jax said, hoping he sounded confident. But would they? Why was he still here if it was the same person? "He figured out who you were," Jax breathed, the final pieces that didn't quite fit falling into place in his mind.

"He figured out that I was the chief of police or that I was Juan's widow?" Keara demanded, sounding like she already knew the answer.

"He was probably planning to move on after the Luna bombing like he had with all the other crimes. But you showed up that night," Jax realized. "Or maybe he followed me when I came to Desparre to talk to you about the case." He told Ben about the blue truck and the agent nodded, jotting notes.

"I'm sorry," he told Keara.

She waved a dismissive hand. "We don't know that was him. And if it was, you shook him. Anyway, if he's sticking around because he realized who I was, that gives us more of a chance to bring him down."

"He's breaking pattern now," Ben said, a warning in his voice that Jax felt deeply himself.

"I know," Keara said, glancing at the other agent. "My husband almost caught him. Maybe he's worried I'm just as good."

"With a personality type like this, if he's breaking pattern, he could be fixating on you," Jax said, the worry he felt coming through in his words.

Keara nodded, fury in her own voice. "He can fixate all he wants. I'm fixated now, too."

"Keara." He stepped closer, trying to block out everyone else, everything else, as she tipped her head up slightly, meeting his gaze.

"I think you could be in danger."

Chapter Eighteen

The air felt stuffy and uncomfortable inside Jax's SUV. Or maybe that was just all of Keara's pent-up anger.

She took a deep breath. The anger and grief over her husband's murder had settled over the years, buried deeper where it was less likely to bubble up at any moment and overwhelm her. But right now, knowing the person who had done it was probably here, trying to destroy the new town she'd chosen to call home, had pushed it all to the surface again, as strong as it had ever been.

It wasn't fair to take it out on Jax.

She glanced at him, saw the worry in his tense profile, in the focused gaze that kept jumping between the dark road ahead and his rearview mirror, like he was watching for a tail. It was obvious he felt guilty, thinking he might have led the bomber to her.

"It's not your fault," she told him.

He glanced at her briefly, pensively, then back out the windshield.

"For all we know, this guy found out where I lived by talking up the locals."

"And no one recognized him?" Jax countered.

"Judging by that sketch, he's not exactly a memorable-looking guy." The couple who'd seen him—assuming the person they'd seen *was* the bomber—said he was just shy of six feet, with thinning brown hair. He'd been wearing a shapeless coat, maybe to disguise his build, and sunglasses on a not-so-sunny day. When asked if there was anything memorable about him, Imani had just shrugged and called him "average."

Keara glanced at Patches in the backseat, sound asleep with her head resting on Keara's overnight bag. "This really isn't necessary." She repeated what she'd said back at her house, when everyone else had either headed home or gone inside to gather evidence. When Jax had insisted she come stay at the hotel where it was safer, she'd rolled her eyes and blurted harshly, "Don't be ridiculous."

Ever the therapist, he hadn't taken offense. Probably he'd recognized her misplaced frustration and fury.

Even now he just said calmly, "We agreed you'd be safer at the hotel. Plus, Patches will love the company."

Woof! she chimed in from the backseat.

Keara twisted to look at the Labrador retriever and couldn't stop her smile. The puppy had been wound up an hour ago, jumping over the seat in Jax's SUV where she'd been shut inside, barking and trying to get someone to let her out. As soon as Keara had given in—and given herself a welcome distraction while federal agents combed through her office, looking for evidence—she'd nudged repeatedly at Keara, like she was mad it had taken so long. Then she'd lain down at Keara's feet and promptly fallen asleep.

She'd been asleep for most of the ride from Keara's house toward the Royal Desparre Hotel, too. But apparently saying Patches's name woke her instantly.

"Can't argue with that, can you?" Jax asked, giving her a tense smile as he pulled into the hotel parking lot.

As he put the SUV in Park and shifted to face her, focusing those compelling deep brown eyes entirely on her, Keara resisted the urge to fidget. She was a police chief. She didn't fidget.

"Jax, look, I don't mean to be rude, but let's be honest here. You're not law enforcement. You can't protect me."

He shrugged, only a brief flicker of offense in his eyes. "Well, then it's a good thing this hotel is full of FBI agents, isn't it?"

"Then what's the point of me staying with you instead of just getting my own room?"

Woof! Woof! Woof! Patches seemed to argue from the backseat.

"If I'm right, then this guy has gotten away with it for at least seven years, Keara," Jax said, sounding tired as he retread the argument they'd already had at her house.

It was an argument he'd won, since she was

here, with her bag packed with her uniform for tomorrow and her work laptop. She'd left her personal vehicle in front of her house, hoping it would seem occupied if the killer decided to return.

Still, the idea that she was leaving the house empty, making it easy for him to go back through it if he wanted, made her antsy. She'd finally agreed to come with Jax when he suggested that if she didn't want to stay with him, she should bunk with one of her officers. The idea of staying with Jax was making her nervous, the attraction between them palpable in the air. But asking one of her officers to lend her their couch felt too close to admitting she wasn't up for being their leader. And that was something she'd never do.

"You know I'm armed," she said once more as he opened the door and started to climb out. "Maybe you don't know this—I'm a damn good shot."

He leaned down, met her gaze with his own less patient one. "Your husband carried a gun, too, right? And this could be the same asshole who killed him, only now he's got seven more years of practice."

Jax held her gaze for a long moment, surely seeing the horror and grief rush across her face at the low blow. Then he stood and shut the door behind him, before opening up the back for Patches.

His dog stared at Keara for a long moment, offered up a *woof!* then climbed out, too.

Keara sat motionless in the SUV, imagining the beautiful sunny day she'd found Juan dead in their backyard. He'd been caught completely by surprise, even when the killer had slipped up right behind him to slit his throat.

Swallowing back the surge of tears that threatened, Keara reached into the back to grab her overnight bag. Then she followed Jax silently into the hotel.

JAX OPENED HIS eyes to find Keara staring at him.

She immediately redirected her gaze, sipping a cup of coffee he'd somehow slept through her brewing. She'd gotten dressed while he was sleeping, too, changing out of the joggers and long T-shirt she'd put on before climbing into the second bed. Now she was wearing her uniform, with the four-star emblem on her collar designating her role as chief of police.

He tore his gaze away from her still-loose hair and makeup-free face to check on Patches. When his dog had realized Keara was staying last night, she'd run in circles for a minute, then leaped onto the bed with Keara and slept at her feet.

His dog was still at the end of the bed, her front paws dangling off the edge. When she saw him looking at her, her tail thumped the bed.

He grinned. He couldn't believe someone had

tossed her out. It was hard not to smile when you saw her. "Hi, Patches."

Throwing off his covers, Jax climbed out of bed and asked, "How did you sleep, Keara?"

He'd zonked out. He wasn't sure how, with the woman he was falling for only a few feet away from him, but it had been a long, stressful day. Apparently, it had caught up to him.

But right now he felt refreshed, reenergized and determined. And the woman he was falling for was still only a few feet away.

Her eyes widened as he stepped closer and she set her coffee down, her mouth moving like she was getting ready to speak.

When he stepped closer still, into her personal space, she surprised him by looping her arms around his neck. "I slept fine. Not quite as well as I did on my couch, though." He could feel her heart rate pick up as she stared at him, giving him a small, sassy grin.

He flashed back to the feel of her spooned against him on her couch and couldn't help but smile back. He wanted to stay in this moment, savor the feeling of being with Keara as if they were a long-established couple and not a pair of colleagues who'd barely known each other more than a week. But her lips were too close to him, her gaze broadcasting a mix of uncertainty and desire.

As he slowly bent his head closer, one of her

hands slid into his hair and the other stroked along the back of his neck, making all of the nerve endings there fire to life. He pressed his lips softly to hers as she sank into him. The gentle meeting of their lips sent sparks through him, but he kept his kiss slow, wanting to linger in the moment.

She tasted like coffee with cream and sugar. She smelled faintly of the lavender soap in the hotel bathroom. She felt exactly right in his arms, like she belonged there.

Too soon, she was pulling back, her gaze serious, despite the passion that still lingered. "Sorry I was hard to deal with yesterday."

He laughed, surprised at the admission. "Thanks for letting me win the argument."

A grin burst on her face, her own laugh soft and short, and somehow, in that moment, he knew. However many dangers she faced because of her job, he still wanted to be with her.

Pulling free of his embrace, she told him, "I may not have known you long, Jax, but I'm figuring you out. And I didn't want you and Patches trying to stand guard at my house." She picked up her brush, started to pull her hair up into its customary work bun. "Much as I appreciate it," she added.

He watched her a minute longer, gave her an easy smile when she glanced questioningly at him. It wasn't time to talk about anything serious. He knew she wasn't ready. But maybe if they could resolve this case, that would change.

Mentally shifting into work mode, he said, "If we assume the killer was planning to stick to pattern and leave after he set the bomb in Luna, that means most likely he spotted you at the scene at some point. Do you think he could have recognized you from Houston?"

Keara froze, one hand holding up all of her long hair, the other holding her brush. Then she continued working it into a bun, her voice steady but underlaid with anger as she replied, "It seems unlikely, but I guess it's possible. More likely he heard my name and recognized that. Then he might have started digging up details on me. There was a picture of me in the paper back in Houston from Juan's funeral. I'm sure that would come up if you dug enough."

"So either he heard someone at the scene say your name or he talked to people, asked who you were," Jax continued, thinking out loud.

"Probably," Keara agreed, jamming bobby pins into her hair and then slapping her hands on her hips. "What are you thinking, Jax?"

At her insistent tone, Patches jumped off the bed, ran to her side and plopped down at her feet, staring up at him, too.

Jax couldn't help another laugh. "Okay, Patches. I'll get to the point." He redirected his attention to Keara. "I'm the one you've had the most contact with from the team in Luna. Maybe the killer followed me, maybe not. But we know he's been paying attention to you. We can assume he knows who I am."

Keara's eyes narrowed. "And..."

"We also know he didn't get any information about the status of the investigation when he broke into your house."

"Assuming this whole theory is right and it was the killer who broke in, then that's true," Keara agreed. "I don't have any information about the bombings—or the killings or arson—at my home."

"So he's still looking for information."

"And you have an idea," Keara said.

"He might have already seen the sketch of himself, so I'm sure he's being careful. Maybe he's tried to change his appearance. But if he's still here, he'll want to find out the status of the case. Who better to get it from than the guy who's been giving *you* information?"

"Okay," Keara said slowly, her narrowed eyes telling him she didn't like where this was headed.

"What if I go back to the scene in Desparre? The FBI has finished processing it, but I've seen residents there every day, leaving signs and stuffed animals for Nate and Talise, looking for information. They all know Patches and I are here to help the victims and the community. We can stick around, let people know we're there for anyone who's struggling to process this, to share what we can about how the investigation is going."

"You hope he'll hear about it and come talk to you," Keara said, her expression telling him she liked this less and less with every word.

"Yes." He stared back at her, trying to project confidence, even though it felt like a long shot. But a long shot was better than nothing.

She started to shake her head and he cut her off. "It's daytime, so there are going to be plenty of people around. He's not going to set off a bomb in the same spot twice."

When she scowled even more at that, he insisted, "Hitting twice in the same state is already a departure for him. Yes, he's been getting away with his crimes for a long time. But that's because he's smart and he's patient. This is a pretty low-risk thing for me to do. It's not really even that far from what I'd normally be doing right now. But maybe it will work. You and some of the agents can set up at a distance and watch. What do you think?"

She sighed and gave him a reluctant-looking nod. "Let's call Ben and get his opinion."

As Jax headed to the bathroom to get changed, he heard her on the phone with the FBI agent. She talked through his idea impartially and fully, even though he knew she would have preferred not to have him involved. But when he stepped out of the bathroom, ready for the day in his standard dark dress pants and a button-up shirt with an FBI jacket over it to let citizens know who he was, she nodded.

"We're on."

Twenty minutes later he was standing next to the temporary short fence that had been erected around the crime scene to keep anyone from hurting themselves before the damage could be repaired. As he looked around the empty scene, Jax wondered if his plan was a mistake.

Three days after the bomb had gone off in Desparre's downtown, people were starting to get back to normal. Instead of congregating near the stash of signs, candles and teddy bears that had been piled high with messages for the dead and wounded in both Desparre and Luna, residents were giving it a wide berth today. Their gazes darted his way briefly, pausing with grief and fear, before they resumed their business. Apparently, they'd hit the point where they hoped to move on, try to forget while they waited for good news on the victims and the suspect's capture.

Jax sighed and knelt next to Patches, who looked as dejected as he felt. She whined a little and he scratched behind her ears.

"I know, Patches. You want to work."

Her tail thumped lightly at the word as she stared up at him, then glanced toward the part of Desparre with all of the shops, with all of the people. It was Sunday morning and in the distance, he could see people in dress clothes starting to stream toward the church down the street from the police station.

His gaze shifted from the far end of town with the church, to a little bit closer, at the police station. From an attic Jax wouldn't have guessed existed in the police building, Keara, Ben and Anderson were watching him through binoculars. So far there was nothing for them to see.

"We'll give it another half hour here, then go find people to talk to," he promised Patches.

Her tail wagged and he grinned at her.

Then dirt sprayed up from the road in front of him, pebbles stinging his legs as a distant *boom* sounded.

For a second he was confused, even as Patches started frantically barking, already standing.

Then the sound registered. Someone had just taken a shot at him. But from where?

Panic followed, tensing his whole body as he glanced around frantically, looking for the shooter, looking for a safe place to go.

Then there was another *boom* like a firecracker going off and a metallic screech as the bullet hit the small fence behind him.

"Run, Patches!" Jax yelled, angling his arm toward downtown. Toward the police station.

She barked, staring up at him, waiting for him, and he took off, too.

He ran as hard as he could, Patches keeping pace at his side, even as he wished for her to out-run him, to get to safety faster.

He was pretty sure the person shooting at him was using a rifle. Which meant either they weren't a great shot or they were playing with him, forcing him to run for his life even though they could end it at any time.

Chapter Nineteen

"Wait!"

Ben's voice echoed behind her as Keara leaped down from the attic in the police station, skipping the entire ladder and landing hard on the floor below.

Pain jolted up from her legs, making her teeth slam together, but she ignored it the same way she ignored Ben. She'd agreed to Jax's plan to try and fool the man who'd killed her husband and now he and Patches were in danger.

She couldn't survive losing another man she loved.

The unexpected thought made grief and dread clamp down hard, almost doubling her over. It was too soon. Way too soon.

"Keara!" Ben yelled. "Get someone up here with a long rifle!"

"Okay," she gasped at him, but she didn't even need to yell the order, because Tate Emory and Charlie Quinn were already rushing toward her, both holding rifles.

They didn't know where the shooter was, but they knew his target.

Maybe she'd make a better one.

There was no time to grab a bulletproof vest, so Keara just straightened and kicked into gear again, running for the front of the station. She blew past her officers, warning them, "Active shooter! Gear up before you come out!" Then she raced outside.

Yanking her pistol from its holster, she ran into the center of the street. Near the church, residents were looking around in confusion and she yelled at them, "Get inside!" Then she spun the other way, toward the park.

Jax and Patches were still running toward her, but there hadn't been any more shots fired. If the killer was smart, he was already trying to disappear. Even with a rifle, there was only so long he could hold off police. They were too close.

They could get him. She could get him.

The thought fueled her, added fury to her fear and determination to her strides, lengthening them even as she kept her gun ready. She'd been one of the best shots in the Houston PD back in the day and she still kept up her practice. If she saw the shooter, he was finished.

As Jax met her gaze, he waved his arm, made a motion at her that clearly meant "turn back."

"Move!" she barked at him as she got close and he started to slow, like he was planning to grab her arm and try to turn her.

His gaze lingered on her, his head pivoting to watch even as he followed her orders and kept going, Patches keeping pace with him.

Then he was behind her and her focus sharpened, her gaze sweeping the empty street in front of her. The killer couldn't be far.

She kept pushing, legs and arms burning as she ran hard toward the park. Her lungs ached, too, out of practice at this kind of running, especially with the chilly Alaskan air sending an icy blast down her throat with every breath. Where would a shooter have the best angle?

As she drew alongside the park, she realized. Down the side street that bisected Main Street, ending just past the park. He'd be able to see Jax, but Jax would be unlikely to see him because the woods continued that way, offering plenty of places to hide.

Boom!

Keara instinctively cringed, even as she dodged left and then right. It wasn't a rifle this time, but the sound of a pistol firing. As she rounded the corner onto the side street, nearly skidding off her feet, she saw him.

About Jax's height, wearing dark green—a good choice to blend into a forest—he was running hard, too. And there was a dark blue truck parked on the street ahead.

She could yell out a warning, shoot him when he inevitably spun and fired at her. Or she could tackle him, bring him in. Force him to admit all the things he'd done, force him to serve time the way he deserved.

Keara hunched inward, pushed her strides as

long as she could, as he slid to a stop alongside his truck, stopping himself by grabbing the side mirror.

Then he was spinning toward her, aiming his gun again.

Keara dove for the ground, twisting as she flew through the air, trying to get her own gun up as another gunshot blasted. She slammed into the hard-packed earth with a grunt that stole all of her air and made her vision momentarily fuzzy.

Then he was in the truck, the tires spitting dirt as she lined up her pistol and fired. She heard the *ping* of her bullet hitting the truck, but it wasn't enough.

The truck careened around the corner and out of sight.

JAX'S HEARTBEAT REFUSED to slow.

He'd been back at the hotel for half an hour, but his body was still amped up, the adrenaline overload not subsiding. He wasn't sure it would until Keara walked through that door and he could see for himself that she was okay.

Kneeling on the floor, he wrapped his arms around Patches's neck, hugging her.

She whined a little, pushed her head up into the crook of his neck. She'd seen a lot of terrible things during her six months as a therapy dog—and she'd definitely had a rough start in life. But she'd never been in danger while she'd worked for the FBI.

Fury and guilt mixed as he stroked the soft fur on her back, whispered, "We're okay, Patches. Keara is okay, too."

She whined again at Keara's name and he knew she had to be wishing for the same thing he was.

As he'd reached the safety of the Desparre police station, a small group of officers had poured outside, wearing bulletproof vests over their uniforms and helmets on their heads. They'd looked serious and nervous, but moved confidently in pairs toward the threat.

Not long afterward, Ben and Anderson had climbed down from the Desparre Police Department's rarely used attic, frowning and shaking their heads. "He got away," Ben had told him. Then he must have seen Jax's panic, because he'd added, "Keara is okay. We're putting out an APB on the truck. Dark blue, like you said."

Now, back in the hotel room where he'd been escorted by a pair of police officers and told to "stay put," Jax wondered: If he'd done something differently when he'd seen that truck, would they have already caught the bomber?

Pushing aside the frustration, he continued to pet Patches until her presence calmed his raging heart. She seemed to relax, too, and she pulled her head off his shoulder to glance at the door.

"I know, Patches. You want Keara."

Her tail wagged and new nerves filled him. Keara hadn't been hurt chasing down the killer, and hopefully they'd get lucky and catch him quickly with the APB. But then he and Patches would be leaving.

He'd been putting off telling her how he felt, putting off telling her that he wanted to pursue a relationship, despite the challenges. He'd been waiting for the right time, hoping this case would end with her getting closure on her husband's murder and make it easier for her to move on. But there was never going to be a perfect time to talk, not even if that happened.

He needed to act.

As if on cue, there was a knock at the door and Patches leaped to her feet, giving an excited bark as her tail whipped back and forth. A reaction like that could only mean one thing: Keara was here.

His heart rate picked up again as he looked through the peephole to confirm it before letting her in.

Keara looked formidable, despite torn sleeves and the dirt covering her once-crisp uniform, despite the strands of hair pulled loose from her bun, and the smear of dirt across one cheek. Determination blazed in her eyes and there was a hard set to her expression that said it didn't matter how far the bomber ran, she was going to find him.

He stood staring at her, watching her gaze run

over him like she was reassuring herself he wasn't injured, as Patches ran in circles around her.

Finally a shaky smile broke and she bent down to pet Patches, before standing and moving closer to him. Close enough to touch, but the intimidating, focused expression was still in her eyes, mixed suddenly with a fear he knew he'd caused.

"Are you okay?" she asked, her voice barely above a whisper.

"We're fine," he reassured her. "I'm not sure he actually wanted to hit us."

She blew out a heavy breath that he felt across his face. "We lost him." She shook her head, and her hard mask broke, showing all the frustration underneath. "The FBI is working with my officers to find him, and we've coordinated with all the surrounding towns to be on the lookout for him or his truck. I got a partial plate, which will help, but…"

She sighed again, ran a hand through her hair that just pulled out more pieces of her bun. "We found the rifle, too, and we're running it for prints. The bastard was wearing gloves, but there's a good chance he loaded it without them, so hopefully we'll get a hit there."

"We'll get him," Jax said, discovering it was easy to inject his voice with confidence. This killer was savvy and he'd gotten away with it for a long time. But the Anchorage agents were very good and very dedicated. And Keara? Jax knew this was the most important case of her life. She wasn't going to rest until she found him. And he'd bet on her over anyone else.

It was something he needed her to know. "Keara—"

"Shh." She put a finger to his lips, then stepped closer. She blinked and the last of the frustration and angry determination faded, leaving behind residual fear and need.

"Are *you* okay?" he asked as he settled his hands on her hips, desperate to pull her to him, desperate to hold her until the threat was gone. But he needed to hear her say it.

"I'm okay now." She pushed his hands aside, unstrapped her holster and set it up on top of his TV. Then she looped her arms around his neck, pushed up on her tiptoes and fused her lips to his.

It was nothing like the kiss they'd shared this morning. Instead of going slow, her grip tightened as soon as his lips started to move against hers. Her tongue breached the seam of his mouth and she moaned, sending his pulse skyrocketing.

Gripping her hips again, harder this time, he pulled her closer until there was no space between them. She was a perfect mix of lean muscle and feminine curves, and her tongue was dancing around the inside of his mouth in a way that made his eyes roll back in his head.

Her kisses were fast and frantic, and Jax met

her pace, learning the curves along her body with his hands as she looped a leg around his hip.

Then she pulled back slightly, breathing heavily, her eyelids at half-mast as she panted, "I can't stay long, Jax. I have to get back out there."

As she was leaning back in, he whispered, "We have all the time we want, Keara. Anchorage and Desparre are only a jumper flight apart." His lips sought hers again, desperate for another feel of her before she went off chasing a killer.

But she pulled away, her hands dropping from around his neck and her leg returning to the floor.

When he opened his eyes, she was still breathing hard, but the desire in her gaze was fading. She nodded, stepping out of his embrace so quickly he almost stumbled, and he tried to figure out what was happening.

"You're right," she said. "And those jumper flights happen every day. The killer has obviously targeted you, Jax, and I don't want it to happen again. You need to get on one as soon as possible. You and Patches should go home."

He stared back at her, his own passion cooling as understanding dawned. Keara wasn't here right now because the overwhelming relief that he was okay had made her realize she wanted something more serious.

She was here to say goodbye.

Chapter Twenty

Patches whined and glanced from Jax to the closed hotel door.

"I know," he said softly, petting her. The look Keara had given them as she'd grabbed her overnight bag and paused at the door, before shutting it softly behind her, was lodged in his brain. It had been full of regret and sorrow. But it had also been full of finality.

She believed he'd follow her advice. She believed she was never going to see them again.

It had been hours since she'd left and he hadn't heard from her since. He knew she was out there somewhere, searching for the bomber. She'd thrown herself into danger while she asked him to run away from it. For the FBI's part, they didn't like that he'd been targeted, either. Ben had called to check in on him. The agent hadn't suggested that he go home, but he'd sounded discouraged as he advised Jax to stay inside.

Jax had agreed, but asked for a favor in return. When Ben had originally run the symbol through the FBI database, they'd focused on the past seven years, since Celia's murder. But today Jax had asked Ben to run the symbol for a ten-year stretch about thirty years ago.

After Keara had left, he'd needed something

else to focus on. Sitting in the quiet of his hotel room with no victims to help and nothing else to do made it too easy to think about the expression on Keara's face as she'd walked out the door. He wasn't about to give up hope of changing her mind.

Still, it was one thing to wish for this case to be solved, for her husband's murder to be solved. For Keara to get closure. He believed in her. She was dogged and a damn good investigator. Maybe it wouldn't happen quickly, but he believed she'd find the person responsible.

But after what happened this morning, he wasn't sure closure would be enough to make her move on. At least not with him.

His job wasn't usually dangerous. Still, he enjoyed using his knowledge of psychology to help investigations. If the opportunity arose again, he didn't want to turn it down. Even if he was willing to promise that, maybe Keara just couldn't bring herself to ever date someone connected to law enforcement again.

He understood it. He'd seen the details from her husband's case file. The murder had been gruesome. He couldn't imagine finding someone he loved that way. He definitely empathized with her need never to lose anyone violently again.

It was why she'd backed away from him. And it wasn't a fear he was sure he could breach, no matter how hard he tried.

Patches whined, nudging his leg, and Jax nodded at her. "You're right. I need to focus."

She slid to the floor, looking dejected, and he wondered if she understood exactly what was happening with Keara, if she was just as upset over it.

Giving her one last pet, he clicked to the next result in the files Ben had sent over. Thirty years ago the FBI's system to compare unsolved crimes was newer. There were fewer entries, so fewer possibilities to go through. But maybe he'd get lucky.

Because the thing he'd realized as he'd tried to find a way to distract himself from Keara's departure was that he'd been right from the very beginning. The symbol meant something. And if it was being used by a single criminal, it was probably connected to that person's childhood.

Working with the victims of a serial killer last year had been brutal. It had taught him that human beings were capable of far worse atrocities than he'd ever seen before up close. It had also taught him that many of the perpetrators came from violence themselves. Instead of learning empathy from it, they'd sought it out, tried to inflict pain on others.

Maybe the bomber was the same. Maybe the symbol came from a traumatic incident in his childhood and he was now marking his own crimes with it. Maybe…

Jax sighed and set aside one more case, wondering if he was wasting time. Even if he was right, the symbol could have been overlooked or never entered in the FBI's voluntary database.

Then his pulse spiked as he flipped to the next case. Here was the symbol he'd seen at two bomb sites, staring back at him from a twenty-nine-year-old case. A murder that had happened in Texas, not far from Houston.

He read fast as Patches sat up, scooting closer and resting her head on his leg. Although the FBI database was meant for unsolved cases, the police in this case had known exactly who the killer was. They just couldn't find him.

Arthur Margrove had been known around the community as a violent man. Prone to picking fights with anyone—including his wife—he'd been arrested repeatedly for assault. He'd served multiple short sentences in jail, but never learned his lesson. After being fired from yet another job, he'd returned to his job site, broken in and smashed everything he could find. Then he'd gone home and murdered his wife.

Today Arthur would be in his sixties. He wasn't the bomber.

But Jax tapped the computer screen, his fingers marking the information he'd been searching for all afternoon and into the early evening. Arthur Margrove had a son.

Todd Margrove had been five years old at the

time of the murder. He'd been standing beside his mother's body when police came looking for Arthur, covered in her blood, probably from trying to help her. Both of them were underneath a bloody symbol drawn on the wall. A symbol that had now been replicated across the country.

Jax grabbed his phone and dialed Keara's number. Frustration gnawed when the call went to voice mail, and he left a tense message:

"Call me back, Keara. I know who the bomber is."

KEARA GLANCED AT the readout on her phone as she drove down the mountain. Jax was calling.

She gripped the wheel tighter as she debated whether to answer. She'd spent the day running leads with her officers, the fury and frustration in her chest building and building until it felt ready to burst.

Nothing was panning out. Thinking about what had happened with Jax in the morning just added fear to the mix.

Whatever Jax wanted now, it wasn't to tell her he'd gone home; she knew that much. She hadn't spoken to him since she'd left his hotel room that morning, but she had talked to the FBI agents, suggesting they get him a flight. Ben had raised his eyebrows at her and told her Jax understood the threat and was staying off the streets. The FBI didn't believe he was in real danger. They thought if the bomber wanted him dead, he wouldn't have missed.

They thought today's shooting was a message. The bomber knew what they were doing and he wasn't falling for it.

He was having fun with them, because after all, if Jax was right, this was what he wanted anyway. A strong opponent to chase him, the thrill of getting away despite their best efforts.

It wasn't going to happen. Not this time.

They might not have prints to give them a name, since the rifle had come up empty. But they had a partial license plate. They had a sketch.

Her phone stopped ringing as Keara rounded another bend, riding the brakes because this stretch of road was steep. She'd gone up to the top of the mountain to talk to the loner who'd been at the scene of the Desparre bombing. He'd called the station and implied he might have seen the person in the sketch. He'd asked for her personally, and because he was a recluse who'd opened up to her in the past, she'd agreed.

Charlie Quinn and his FBI partner had spoken to him yesterday and reported back that he was crotchety and uncooperative, but didn't have any useful information. It seemed unlikely he'd have something new today, but she had to check. Plus, it gave her some time to herself.

But when she'd arrived, no matter how many ways she asked, the information he'd claimed to have didn't surface. Instead, he'd spent the entire discussion digging for details on the case. Maybe it was because he'd suffered some minor injuries, cuts to his legs that had required stitches. Or maybe he was just one of those guys who got off on crime scene details.

He wasn't the bomber. In his late fifties, in poor health and bad shape, not only did he not fit the description, but he'd lived in Desparre too long.

Still, Keara's radar was up. As soon as she'd returned to her SUV, she'd called the station to update them, let them know she was heading back in.

The whole thing had been a waste of time. Peering up at the sky through her windshield, she scowled at the fading light filtering through the towering trees. Pretty soon it would be dark. Her officers had been working a lot of overtime in the past four days. The shooting downtown today meant they'd needed to spend as much time reassuring the public and keeping a visible presence there as running leads.

The more time that passed from when the bomber had shown up in the park, the farther he could run. Yes, he'd found a police department— and a group of federal agents—to try and outwit. But he hadn't made it so many years without being caught by being stupid. Maybe the shots at Jax had been his parting ones. His way of telling them they'd gotten as close as they ever would. His own form of goodbye, before he showed up in some other state, committed some other crime.

Rounding another corner, Keara's SUV jolted as it ran over something in the road. The back of her vehicle did the same and then the tires started making a rhythmic *thump thump thump*.

Flat tires.

What the hell had she hit?

Glancing around her at the darkening woods, Keara put her SUV in Park and pulled her gun as she stepped out of the vehicle.

Scanning the area and seeing nothing unusual, she walked to the back of her vehicle. There was a plank of wood driven through with upward facing nails directly behind her back wheels.

Adrenaline rushed through her, all her senses on alert as she lifted her weapon. She spun around just as something flew toward her head.

Keara ducked, trying to center her weapon at the figure that had rushed out of the woods, but the slab of wood still made contact with the top of her head.

Pain exploded in her skull, bringing tears to her eyes. Her feet came out from underneath her and her arm slammed down on the edge of the board of nails, making her lose her grip on the gun. It skidded away from her, out of reach.

Then the man she'd seen only from a distance that morning was filling her vision, a smile on his face. The bomber, murderer, arsonist. The man who'd shot at Jax. The man who'd killed Juan.

He wavered in her sight, her vision blurry from the hit to the head, her lungs screaming from the hard landing. Fighting the urge to throw up, ignoring the burning pain in her arm, Keara shoved herself upward, launching at him.

But he moved fast, swinging that slab of wood again.

Even though she threw up her arm to block it, the wood still made contact with the side of her head.

She hit the ground again, head throbbing, nausea welling up hard.

Then she was moving, her head bumping over every uneven piece of ground, into the woods.

Her vision went in and out, as dizziness threatened to overtake her, threatened to suck her into unconsciousness. Panic erupted, flooding her system with terror, but keeping her awake. She was weak from the blows to her head, too dizzy to stand. Too dizzy to fight.

He left her for a moment and she swallowed the nausea, tried to move, but her body wouldn't cooperate. Then the bushes in front of her were moving and she blinked, trying to right her swaying vision, until she realized it wasn't bushes she was seeing.

They were camouflage, broken branches strategically covering the truck he'd hidden just off the road. He planned to put her in that truck, to take her somewhere else.

It wasn't a quick death he planned for her, but probably a painful one.

Keara rolled onto her belly, biting down on her cry of pain as her vision swung one way and then back again and her head throbbed violently. *Where was her gun?*

Too soon it didn't matter because she was being lifted, thrown over his shoulder with frightening ease. He carried her around to the back of the truck where a metal gun box was propped open.

Keara kicked, raking her fingernails over the backs of his arms, still coherent enough to think like the cop she was. To get his DNA on her.

He yelped and swore and then he was swinging her fast enough to make her nausea overwhelming, make her vomit on the ground beneath him. Soon the ground disappeared altogether and she was being stuffed into the empty gun box.

She shoved upward, trying to escape, but he'd dropped her into the box awkwardly, making it hard to move. The multiple blows to the head and the new wave of dizziness slowed her down, too. The lid closed, leaving her in darkness.

As she heard him move away from her, she took deep breaths to reduce her panic, then slammed against the metal lid, trying to open it. The lid buckled slightly, but held. Then the truck started to move, taking her away with Juan's killer.

Chapter Twenty-One

"Have you heard from Keara?" Jax asked Ben over the phone, trying not to give in to worry. He'd called the agent after Keara hadn't picked up, and told him the same news he'd given Keara's voice mail.

"No. She's on her way back from talking to someone up the mountain. She got a weird vibe from it, though. Said she'd stay in touch on her way down." There was a pause and Jax imagined Ben frowning at his watch. "If I don't hear from her in the next ten minutes, I'll give her a call."

Could she have followed a trail right to the bomber's home? Or maybe he'd followed her up there, ambushed her on her way back?

Jax only halfway paid attention as Ben went on about what a great find Jax had made and said he'd start running the name Todd Margrove immediately. Then he asked if Jax thought it was Rodney's elusive roommate from back in Texas. From the way he asked, Jax had a feeling he'd repeated the question a few times.

"Yeah, maybe. Look, let me call you back, okay?" He hung up without waiting for an answer, dread forming in his gut.

Maybe he was overreacting because he'd been shot at that morning, but he suddenly couldn't stop picturing Keara in trouble. "Come on, Patches. Let's go for a drive."

Woof! She leaped to her feet, danced around him even as she didn't get the usual laugh out of him.

He moved faster the closer he got to his SUV, scanning the semidarkened parking lot. He opened the back door and Patches jumped in, then Jax got behind the wheel.

"Hold on, Patches," he told her, driving faster than was legal as he whipped out of the parking lot and headed for the mountain. It was closer from here than the police station and he couldn't wait the ten minutes for Ben to follow up with Keara, then call back and tell Jax he was overreacting.

He could hear Patches sliding around a bit in the backseat as he rushed toward the base of the mountain, where the main road led up to the best place in Desparre to hide out. But were there other roads off it? He had no idea.

"Sorry, Patches," he told her, wondering if he should have left her in the hotel room. But most likely he *was* overreacting. And if he caught up to Keara coming down the mountain, maybe she'd be more open to talking with an adorable dog begging for her attention, too.

"Almost there," he muttered a few minutes later as the road that led off the mountain came into sight.

Before he reached it, a dark blue truck sped away, making a turn in the opposite direction Jax was coming from.

It was *the* truck.

Jax's pulse picked up as he instinctively punched down harder on the gas. Had Keara run into the bomber on the mountain? Had he hurt her? Was she still up there?

Yanking his phone out of his pocket, he told it, "Call Ben Nez!"

As he reached the base of the mountain, Jax's gaze pivoted from the road that went up the mountain to the street heading out of Desparre that the blue truck had taken. Should he go search for Keara up the mountain? Or follow the bomber?

He clenched his teeth, panicked at the thought of making the wrong choice. *Go after the bomber.* It was Keara's voice in his head. He could imagine her insisting she could take care of herself, to keep the bomber in sight and get the police and FBI on him now.

"Ben here. What is it, Jax?"

The way Ben said his name, the stress in his voice, told Jax he'd repeated himself again.

"I found the bomber. Coming down off the mountain in that same truck. He's heading out of town. I'm following him." Jax's voice sped up as he made his decision. He passed the road up the mountain, hoping he'd made the right choice.

"*What?* Jax, where are you exactly?" Ben asked.

Jax gave him the road, then demanded, "Did you hear back from Keara?"

There was a pause that made dread drop to Jax's stomach, then Ben admitted, "She's not answering her phone. Anderson and I were just about to head up the mountain."

"Should I turn around?" Jax demanded, trying not to panic. Maybe Keara couldn't answer because the roads were dark. He'd heard agents the other day complaining about how narrow they were, how the sudden drop-offs alongside the road in places were startling. Maybe she didn't want to dig her phone out of her pocket and be distracted from driving.

"No," Ben insisted. "Stay on the bomber. Just make sure you stay at a distance. You don't want this guy spotting you, okay? Just stick behind him and keep giving us updates. We're on our way."

"No," Jax insisted. "Send someone else. You need to go find Keara."

"Jax, if Keara's in trouble, it's probably connected to that truck," Ben said, his tone darkly serious, noises in the background suggesting he was already heading for his vehicle. "But we'll send officers up the mountain just in case. We're coming to you. Just be safe. The road you're on leads out of Desparre. It eventually goes into a neighboring town so small they don't even have their own police department. What they do have is a lot of secluded, wooded areas where a bomber might hide. One of Keara's officers was just talking about it earlier today as a place where the bomber could be if he wasn't in Desparre or Luna."

"Okay," Jax agreed, only half listening as he focused on the road ahead. It was empty except for him and the blue truck. He didn't want to get too close and tip the bomber off that he was being followed. He also didn't want to lag too far behind, have the guy take a sudden turn and disappear before Jax could catch up.

"This guy is a killer, Jax," Ben stressed, as if Jax needed the reminder.

He knew all too well what the bomber had done to Keara's husband, what he'd done to Keara's life.

"If you think he's spotted you, turn around. Give us his last coordinates and we'll be right behind him," Ben insisted. "Don't risk your life. You're not an agent. You're not trained for this. Do you hear me? You do *not* want to end up alone with this guy."

"Okay," Jax agreed, not sure if he meant it. Where was Keara? Why hadn't she called him back? Why hadn't she answered Ben's calls?

"Shit," he swore as the truck suddenly sped up, whipping off the road and onto a bisecting trail into the woods.

Jax hit the gas, and as he headed farther away from town, Ben's voice came through a burst of static. "Jax! Did you hear me? Don't engage!"

From the backseat, Patches yelped as she slid across the seat.

"Hang on, Patches," he said, slowing as he reached the turn the blue truck had taken. He eased off the gas entirely, until his SUV was just creeping forward, until he could crane his head and stare down the road.

Boom!

Jax punched the gas again as the gunshot blasted, and his SUV raced forward. Hopefully, they'd pass the road before the bomber could hit them. Hopefully, the bomber wouldn't follow, but would use that opportunity to keep going.

Patches yelped again as Jax gripped the wheel hard, ducking his head low, hoping neither of them would be a visible target.

But as they passed the trail, the truck was still stopped, the brake lights lit up. A hand disappeared back inside the driver's side window, and the truck started up again as if the driver was going to take this chance to get away.

He had a brief instant of relief. Then the gun box in the back of the truck popped open and Keara partially emerged from it.

KEARA GASPED IN the cool night air as she finally got the lid free. She pushed herself upward, desperate to get out of the box that had felt like a too-small coffin.

Ironically, it had been the truck slamming to a

stop after taking that nausea-inducing turn that had given her the right angle, just enough leverage, to shove open the box. Now she ducked low again as the unmistakable sound of a bullet pierced the air.

Was he shooting at her?

As quickly as the thought entered her head, she realized it was wrong. The bomber was shooting at Jax, who was amazingly behind them. His SUV had been racing past the trail where they were stopped, but then his eyes widened in the window, his expression caught in the glow from the bomber's brake lights.

Jamming the box lid fully upward, Keara pushed unsteadily to her feet, ready to leap out and race for Jax's SUV.

Then the bomber hit the gas.

Her upper body went flying forward, wrenching her mostly out of the box and into the truck bed. The metal lid of the box slammed against her calves, but she barely felt the pain over the jolt to the rest of her body as she landed hard, then slid toward the edge where the back of the truck bed had popped open.

Catching herself before she slid right out, Keara grabbed the edge, holding on. Her fingers sliced open on the metal as she held on hard, as she tried to angle her legs to brace herself against the side. She eyed the ground below, moving rapidly enough to intensify her dizziness. They were going too fast. She'd missed her chance to jump.

Then Jax's SUV backed up and spun wildly onto the road, chasing them.

The truck jerked to the side and Keara lost her grip on the edge as she flew sideways across the truck bed. She slammed into the side of it, grabbing the edge there as her body spun and her legs dangled off the vehicle, hanging in midair. Head pounding, she scrambled to get fully back on the truck as it swerved again and the *boom* of a bullet fired.

Maneuvering onto her knees, she peered into the front of the truck, where the bomber leaned out the window, slowing slightly as he fired backward at Jax.

Gritting her teeth, Keara pulled herself slowly, painfully, up the truck bed, smearing blood in her wake. Could she get to the left side, near the front of the truck bed? Could she reach the bomber's hand, yank the gun free? Shooting him while she was in the bed of his moving truck wasn't her best plan, but it didn't seem like her worst option, either.

The truck sped up again and Keara's knees slid out from underneath her. She swore as she slammed against the truck bed again, and her arms were yanked hard as she kept her grip on the side. Ignoring the sharp ache in her arms and shoulders, Keara kept dragging herself forward.

She glanced back and saw Jax gaining. She wanted to tell him to get off this trail, get himself out of danger, but she was also grateful for the backup, grateful that she wasn't completely alone with a practiced killer.

Taking deep breaths to try to ease the pounding in her head and the throbbing across her entire body, Keara grabbed the front of the gun box. Painfully, far slower than she would have liked, she moved on her knees across the front of the truck bed, pulling herself with her bloodied hands.

When she was halfway there, the bomber twisted to look at her. His eyes inches from hers through the glass startled her, almost made her lose her grip.

There was a darkness in his gaze Keara had never seen before in over a decade of policing, a fury to his scowl that said he was going to make her pay for daring to go up against him.

Keara glared right back, refusing to show him any fear. Today this ended. And it wouldn't be with her painful death. It would be with his arrest.

Lurching sideways, Keara made it to the left side of the truck. Adrenaline or determination was helping her vision even out, pushing the pounding in her head to the background. Now that he knew she'd gotten free of the gun box, would he hold his pistol out the window again?

Would he be expecting her to make a grab for it and not take the risk? Or would he focus it on her?

Glancing behind her, she saw Jax. He was gaining on them, close enough now that she could make out the grim determination on his face.

Then the bomber hit the gas again, hard.

Keara swore as her knees came out from under her once more and she banged into the edge of the gun box headfirst, slicing a cut across her forehead. Holding on tighter to the side, she scrambled, trying to wedge her legs against the front and side of the truck. No way could she let go at such a high speed, with the way he kept wrenching the wheel back and forth slightly. No way could she make a grab for his gun if he tried to fire at Jax again.

But from the corner of her eye, she saw Jax getting closer. He was almost on top of them now, gesturing for her to do…what? Try to jump onto the front of his SUV? She shook her head at him, knowing that was a move made for movies, and would probably be deadly at this speed.

Then the bomber slammed on the brakes and Keara's grip came loose from the truck edge. She was thrown against the front of the truck and the gun box, but barely felt the pain as she twisted toward Jax, and the SUV still racing for her.

He was going to hit the truck. At that speed, with that much force, it would probably kill her.

She took a deep breath and tried not to show

any fear as she stared back at the man she'd somehow fallen for in such a short time.

It felt like everything was moving in slow motion as his eyes went huge, then his jaw clamped down.

The SUV wrenched sideways as Jax must have yanked the wheel hard. The right wheels came off the ground and for a terrifying moment, she thought he was going to flip it. Then the SUV came back down again and he must have hit the brakes. But not hard enough, because the front of the SUV slammed into one of the trees lining the trail and the whole front of the vehicle crumpled inward.

"No!" Keara screamed as the bomber hit the gas again, and she went flying to the back of the truck.

She grabbed hold before she was tossed over the edge, her hands shaking with the desire to let go, let momentum carry her. But if the fall didn't kill her, the bomber would surely get out and finish the job while she was incapacitated or out cold.

Praying that Jax had survived the crash, Keara stared at the SUV, hoping to see him climb out. But all she could see was smoke billowing from the front of the vehicle, and then too soon, the bomber turned off onto another trail.

Trying to push Jax to the back of her mind, Keara scanned the truck bed, searching for something she could use as a weapon. But there was nothing here. The gun box had been empty, too. But it was old, dented from her twisting inside it and slamming her boots into the lid. Could she rip it off? It wasn't much, but it was better than nothing.

Before she could even start to pull herself back to the front of the truck, the bomber slowed and then came to a stop.

Shoving herself to her feet, Keara glanced over the top of the truck at a tiny cabin, tucked deep into the woods. Swearing, she leaped off the truck, ready to make a run for it.

Too fast, she heard the truck door open behind her and the bomber snapped, "Do it and I shoot you in the back."

A small part of her, knowing it was probably the least painful way to go, wanted to do it anyway. But that wasn't her. She was a fighter, right to the end.

Gritting her teeth, she turned toward him.

He laughed, surprise evident in the sound. "That was a rougher ride than I thought, wasn't it?"

Ignoring the jibe, she tried to throw him off guard, give him a reason to think she was still a worthy opponent, not worth killing yet. "So where's Rodney Brown? Is this all your doing or are you two working together?"

He let out another sound, somewhere between

a laugh and a grunt, and his gun lowered to his side. "Rodney has been dead for seven years."

Surprise jolted through her as he continued, "I borrowed his car when I killed Celia Harris. You know I did that, right?" He nodded, a slight smile forming. "I didn't expect anyone to come looking for the car. Rodney was belligerent with the cop, of course, and I couldn't take any chances."

Pain and anger filled her, overriding her physical pain as he spoke of her husband.

His smile grew, as if he could see it. "Rodney has been dead since the day that cop— your husband, right?—came to the house. I dumped his body in the ocean. Then I tracked down the cop and slit his throat."

Keara felt herself sway at the words, felt a familiar, incapacitating grief rip through her as the bomber shrugged and added, "And then I moved on."

He lifted his gun again as she tried to breathe through the pain. "And I'll tell you, you've been a lot of fun, but it's getting a bit dicey for me here. I think it's time for me to move on again."

Chapter Twenty-Two

Something was burning.

Jax groaned and lifted his head off the steering wheel, not sure if he'd blacked out or if he'd just hit his head when he'd slammed his SUV into the tree, trying to avoid smashing into Keara.

Keara!

Opening his eyes, he saw nothing but white. The airbag had deployed. He groaned again as he twisted his head, peering around it out the side window. The truck was gone.

Woof!

Jax whipped around in his seat, and his chest and shoulder screamed in protest. "Patches! Are you okay?"

She whimpered and he cursed himself for having brought her along.

"I'm sorry, Patches. I'm coming." He tried to smash the airbag out of his way and the movement sent a tearing pain through his left arm. Cursing, he unhooked his belt and twisted, ignoring the way his shoulder screamed as he slid out from behind the airbag.

Peering into the backseat, he saw his dog on the floor. She stood when he met her gaze, her tail wagging slowly, pointing downward.

"Are you okay, Patches?" He reached back with

his right hand, letting his left arm hang limply. Had it been wrenched out of the socket in the crash? He wasn't sure.

When he pet Patches, she leaned closer, stretching her head between the seats and licking his face.

His gaze ran over her, searching for injuries, but she looked okay. Then she leaped up, putting her front paws between the seats, and relief filled him. If she could move like that, she probably hadn't broken anything.

Resting his head on hers for a second, Jax tried to take deep breaths. It hurt his chest a little, but he was pretty sure it was the way he was twisted, pain radiating from his shoulder.

Then the hint of smoke hit him again and he spun forward, peering out the front. There was a lot of smoke coming out of his vehicle, but he didn't see fire.

The whole front of the vehicle was smashed in. Would it still drive?

He turned the key, giving it a try even though it seemed pointless. It didn't even make a noise.

Swearing, he slid over to the passenger side and opened the door. He half fell, half climbed out of the SUV and then Patches was outside next to him, having leaped over the seats.

How far had the bomber taken Keara? And where was his backup? Had they driven right past this trail, sticking to the road Jax had given Ben on the phone?

Jax stuck his head back into the SUV, fumbling around for his phone, which had been in the center console. When he finally found it underneath the passenger seat, he discovered the screen was smashed. He tried turning it on anyway, but nothing happened.

"Damn it!" Heaving out a sigh, Jax glanced back toward the road he'd followed the bomber down, the road that presumably his backup would be rushing to. Then he looked the other way, in the direction the bomber had probably taken off.

How far had he gone? Jax could see another trail bisecting this one up ahead, but the trail he was on continued as far as he could see, too. The sun was very low in the sky now, casting pinks, oranges and yellows over the tops of the trees. He wasn't sure where he was or where exactly this trail led. But it was going to be completely dark soon and one thing he did know: they were far from help.

Woof! Patches ran down the trail slightly, then glanced back at him, barking again.

"You want to find Keara?"

Woof!

Jax nodded. Hurrying to the back of his SUV, he grabbed the tire iron that had been useless the last time he'd pulled it out. But it was the closest thing he had to a weapon. Not much use against a gun, but better than nothing.

Then he jogged after Patches, breathing through the pain that rattled in his head each time he put his foot down, and the sharp ache that kept searing through his left arm.

She stayed ahead of him, glancing back periodically to make sure he was following. When she reached the connected trail, she turned onto it without hesitation.

Jax followed, his heart thumping harder from adrenaline and pain, but also fear of what was up ahead. Was Keara here? Was he already too late to help her?

He jogged forward a few more steps, caught up to where Patches had stopped to stare back at him. And then he saw it. A driveway with a dark blue truck in it. Behind that, a small wood cabin.

Putting his finger to his lips, he knelt beside Patches and whispered, "Shhh." He glanced at the drive again, searching for any sign of Keara or the bomber, but he didn't see either one.

Hugging his good arm around Patches, he kissed the top of her head, then stood. Angling his arm back the way they'd come, he told her, "Go back to the car, Patches. Wait there."

She glanced behind her, then stared up at him, confusion in her soft brown eyes.

"I need you to go back to the car," he repeated, knowing she understood the word. Eventually,

Ben and Anderson would find his vehicle, even if they needed to contact the rental company and run a trace on it. If Jax was dead by then, he knew the agents would find Patches a good home.

"I love you, Patches. You're such a good girl," he told her, trying not to let his voice crack.

She sat down and he shook his head, angling his hand again.

"Go, Patches," he said, then turned away from her, creeping toward the cabin. He knew she didn't want to do it, but she *was* a good girl. She'd go and at least she'd be safe.

Taking deep breaths, Jax tried to block everything out: fear for Patches, fear for himself, fear for Keara. He tried to just focus on his surroundings as he crept up to the cabin.

They were inside. They had to be.

Praying that Keara was still alive, Jax slunk up to the edge of the cabin. The windows at the front were totally covered, so he slid along the side of the house, searching for a view inside, some idea of what he was getting himself into.

Feeling hyperattuned to every sound, Jax cringed as dead leaves from last fall crunched lightly under his feet. The edges of fir trees brushed against him as he crept alongside the cabin. His adrenaline was pumping hard, but he felt focused. He gripped the wrench harder, hoping he'd be able to use it.

Then he came up to another window, with a

small space where the curtain hadn't been fully shut. Inside the cabin the bomber was standing with his back partially to Jax, a gun held loosely at his side. Across from him, Keara was swaying on her feet, blood on her forehead and her uniform, a dark bruise across her cheek. But she was alive. And she looked fighting mad.

Relief and fury mingled, and Jax picked up his pace, slipping around to the back of the house. There was a door here.

Jax tested the handle and it turned under his hand. Heart pounding, he eased the door open and slid inside.

The bomber didn't turn. If Keara saw him, she gave no indication of it.

Taking light, careful steps, Jax moved forward. His breath was shallow as he tried not to make a sound, as he lifted the wrench, got it in position to smash it down across the back of the bomber's head.

One more step…

The bomber spun toward him, gun lifting fast, a smile rushing over his face. "Welcome to the party."

JAX WAS HERE.

Keara tried not to look past the bomber as he stared at her, snarling the way he'd been doing for the past few minutes. She'd thought he was going to shoot her on the driveway, but then a distant noise had made him frown and usher her inside.

Since then he'd bragged about paying off the loner on top of the mountain, laughed at the police response to his Desparre bomb. He'd done it all with a slight smile hovering on the corner of his lips, like he was hoping she'd rush him. Hoping to infuriate her before he shot her.

She'd gritted her teeth and stared back at him with as unaffected a look as she could manage. But she'd known he was just working himself up to something she couldn't withstand. He was working himself up to Juan's murder. Maybe to Jax's, too, if he hadn't made it out of that SUV.

But now Jax was here. Alive and somehow in this cabin.

Just as he raised a big metal wrench over his head and Keara thought it was all about to end, the bomber spun and told Jax, "Welcome to the party."

Keara wouldn't have dared trying to rush the bomber when he was that close to Jax, the gun pointed. But he spun back to keep them both in his eye line quickly.

The bomber shook his head, said to Jax in a mock-sad tone, "And here I let you live at the park." But he couldn't seem to stop a smile from breaking.

Jax slowly lowered the wrench, dropped it to the floor with a *clang* that made Keara flinch.

"If you killed me, then how would I be able to rue how much smarter you are than me?" Jax asked, his tone and expression even.

The bomber's eyes narrowed, like he wasn't sure if Jax was mocking him. Then he shrugged and said, "Like I told Keara, you've given me some fun here. I like a challenge. But the heat is getting a little too close. It's about time for me to move on. And I'm afraid you can't come with me."

"Where to next, Todd?" Jax asked.

Keara's attention jolted from Jax to the bomber, who visibly jerked.

Then he gave a forced smile. "You're better than I thought you were. How'd you get my name?"

"An old case," Jax said and the bomber's eyes narrowed as he shifted more to face Jax, his gun lowering slightly as he took his attention mostly off Keara.

Her breath stalled. She had no idea how Jax had come up with Todd's name, with details of his past. But if Jax could keep Todd talking, keep his attention, maybe she could rush him. She wasn't at full strength—not even close—but she had rage and desperation on her side. She would *not* watch another man she loved die.

"How old?" Todd asked, his voice squeaking slightly.

"Twenty-nine years old," Jax replied evenly,

his gaze never shifting to her. "Committed by your father."

Todd scoffed. "He was no *father*."

"Then why use his symbol?" Jax asked. "Why repurpose it as your own?"

Todd grinned slowly, and the evil there made a shiver race over Keara's skin.

"That might have been his kill, but it's always been my symbol."

"You smeared your mother's blood on the wall?" Jax asked, surprise in his voice that told Keara he hadn't found all of the answers. "Why?"

Todd scowled, shook his head. Something in his expression told Keara even he wasn't sure of the answer. "Does it matter? That's my symbol."

"And what about the man who killed your mother? It didn't bother you that people thought it was his symbol?" Jax asked.

Keara slid forward, one tiny millimeter at a time, holding her breath, trying not to listen too closely to the horrible tale of Todd's childhood. She needed to get close enough to launch herself at him and she needed him to be distracted enough that she'd land before he could lift his gun and fire. But she had to be completely focused.

"I dealt with him. Right before I killed Celia Harris," Todd said, his head tipping up, pride and hate in his words.

Jax nodded slowly, not looking afraid. "It gave you the courage to try a riskier kill."

Todd scowled again. "I didn't need courage, but yeah, I went for someone people would actually miss." He shrugged, then gave a broad grin that told Keara she needed to move soon. "And then I discovered how much *fun* it was to fool the police."

He started to turn back toward her and she knew: this might be her only chance.

But he was twisting too fast, his gun lifting again.

She wouldn't make it. But she had to try.

Keara launched herself off the ground even as Jax's "Keara, no!" rang out and Todd's smile shifted into a sinister smirk.

A familiar *woof! woof! woof!* came from behind Jax and a blur of brown and black fur raced through the doorway.

Todd's smirk slipped as he twisted back in the other direction.

Then Keara landed hard, roping her arms around Todd, trapping him beneath her as they hit the ground. The force of it reverberated through her body as she focused on his gun hand. Ignoring the searing pain in her own hands, the slippery blood making it hard to hold on, she gripped his middle fingers and twisted them backward.

He yelped and lost his grip on the gun.

Keara shoved it away from him as she leveraged herself into a crouched position over him, yanking his arms up behind his back like she was going to cuff him.

Before she could, he rolled, shoving her off him.

Then he was pushing himself off the ground.

"I wouldn't do that," Jax said, his voice low and deadly.

Keara glanced up.

Jax stood with his feet braced apart like he was on a firing range, the pistol in one hand as the other arm dangled strangely at his side. Patches stood beside him, her teeth bared in a way Keara had never seen.

Todd lowered himself back down and then the room erupted in noise as the front door crashed inward and Ben and Anderson rushed inside.

"You're under arrest," Ben yelled, weapon directed at Todd as Anderson yanked Todd's hands up behind his back and cuffed him.

Jax lowered the pistol he held and gave Keara a shaky smile.

It was over.

Epilogue

A week later Keara stood in front of her officers in the Desparre Police Department, trying not to choke up. "It's been an honor working with all of you for the past six years," she told them.

They stared back at her, giving each other uncertain looks, not having expected this speech on her first day back in the office.

She'd spent the past week at home recuperating. Although the most concerning of her injuries had been the repeated hits she'd taken to her head, everything had looked normal on all the tests. It was the small puncture wounds across her arm from the nail board, her sliced-open hands from hanging on to the edge of the truck and the split on her forehead requiring stitches that had actually kept her away longest.

"Desparre has truly become a home to me," she continued, wanting to get it all out before she became overemotional. "It's going to be hard to leave."

"You're leaving?" Nate Dreymond asked, surprise and disappointment in his tone.

He wasn't officially back on duty yet and wouldn't be for a few weeks, at least. But ever since he'd been released from the hospital, he'd come in each day to see his colleagues.

Talise, too, had woken from her coma. She was still in the hospital, but doctors expected her to make a full recovery.

The town was moving forward. With Todd Margrove behind bars and expected never to be free again, it was going to help everyone heal. Including her.

"It's time," she told them, even though she'd never expected to be leaving the place that had given her so much after Juan died. It had given her a reason to live again, a purpose to help her move on. And it had led her to Jax.

She glanced behind her, where Jax and Patches stood in the doorway. Patches was fidgeting, more full of puppy energy than Keara was used to, her tail thumping whenever Keara glanced her way. Jax was more subdued, his arm still in a sling, the sympathy in his gaze lending her strength.

He knew this wasn't easy for her. But she'd come back to Desparre someday, to see the people and the place that had changed her life.

"Where are you going?" The way Tate's gaze shifted briefly to Jax when he asked it, he probably already knew.

"I'm moving to Anchorage. I'm going to be a detective again."

She'd officially had her interview over the phone two days ago, gotten the call that they wanted her yesterday. It probably hadn't hurt that a longtime agent of the FBI had contacted them and said they'd be crazy not to hire her.

The officers glanced at each other again, and she could feel the mix of emotions in the room: still some confusion and sadness, but they were happy for her, too.

Technically, being a detective was a step down. And moving across the state, to a place where she barely knew anyone, was definitely a sacrifice.

It was also fast. Fast enough that it scared her a little. If she was being honest with herself, it scared her a lot.

She'd known Juan for more than a year before they started dating, had been with him for nearly three years before they got married. But she'd only spent a year as his wife before losing him.

She didn't want to waste any time with Jax, didn't want to look back and have regrets. Not everyone got a second chance like this and she wasn't going to let it go because she was afraid.

She hadn't wanted to fall for him. Hell, she hadn't wanted to fall for anyone, especially not someone who was remotely in harm's way. And despite Jax's official title, he was too good at psychoanalysis to stay completely removed from the investigative side of things. He would never be one hundred percent safe.

Then again, no one was.

"Congratulations," Charlie said, his voice booming over the silence that had fallen.

Then all of her officers were chiming in, offering her congratulatory handshakes and hugs.

Twenty minutes later she walked to the door, giving the room one last, long look. She wasn't officially leaving for a few weeks. She was going to help find her replacement, so she wouldn't leave the town she loved in a lurch. But today felt like goodbye.

As she reached him, Jax took her hand and she smiled at him. Today also felt like a new beginning.

Woof! Patches said and Keara laughed, bending down to pet her. Then she stood and took Jax's hand again.

"Are you sure this is what you want?" Jax asked as they stepped outside into the brilliant sunshine. "You know I'm willing to do any amount of jumper flights. Patches and I can try to be here every weekend if you want to stay."

He gestured at the police station where she'd spent so many of her waking hours in the past six years. "I know these people have become like family to you."

Keara squeezed his hand tighter. "I've loved being a chief. And you're right, I'm going to really miss everyone in Desparre. But being a detective is in my blood."

She let out a cleansing breath. "After Juan's murder went cold, I didn't want to do it anymore. Every part of being a detective was just a reminder that he didn't have any justice. But I'm ready now."

She stared up at him, knowing he could probably read her nervousness in her smile. "I want to do it near you. If you don't think it's too soon."

"Too soon?" He laughed. "I was ready to profess my love a week ago."

She felt herself jerk slightly, at the surprise of his words, at the fear they evoked inside her. But she pushed the fear down. There were no guarantees in life, but Jax had faced down a murderer for her. They'd both come out of it alive. And for as long as they both had left, she wanted to be with him.

A grin burst free, the fear suddenly overrun by an absolute certainty that she was doing the right thing. "I love you, too, Jax."

Woof!

Keara laughed, the sound louder and more gleeful than expected, as she bent to scratch Patches's ears. "I love you, too, Patches."

As she stood again, still holding tight to Jax's hand, he tugged her toward the park. Work was already well underway to return it to its previous state.

Keara took a deep breath of the crisp, clean Alaskan air and glanced around at Desparre's downtown. People were walking around, smiling and laughing, unafraid.

Then she turned back to Jax, the last of her

fear fading into the background. She was ready to live that way, too.

She was ready to forge a new future, with him and Patches.

* * * * *